OVERWHELMING ~~ACCLAIM FOR~~
GENE BREWER AND **K-PAX**

"Throughout, the narrator's matter-of-fact, clinical tone makes this touching and suspenseful story all the more convincing." —*Publishers Weekly*

"[A] fascinating novel." —*Booklist*

"A fine and fantastic story, suitable and very highly recommended for everyone from teens to adults." —*Library Journal*

"Compelling and intelligently crafted." —*Time Out*

"Genuinely funny and touching." —*San Francisco Examiner & Chronicle*

"A fascinating, off-beat novel that is unexpectedly entertaining." —*Detroit News*

"[A] cleverly structured and impressively well-written story ... Fiction or not, Brewer stretches your senses." —*Cleveland Plain Dealer*

"Delightful ... with *K-PAX* Brewer shows us that there is more than one way to have a happy ending and that there is no reason why reality can't meld to fit everyone." —*Southern Book Trade*

"A snappy and enthralling little fantasy." —*The Guardian*

ALSO BY GENE BREWER

K-PAX

ON
A BEAM
OF
LIGHT

Gene Brewer

St. Martin's Paperbacks

NOTE: If you purchased this book without a cover you should be aware that this book is stolen property. It was reported as "unsold and destroyed" to the publisher, and neither the author nor the publisher has received any payment for this "stripped book."

ON A BEAM OF LIGHT

Copyright © 2001 by Gene Brewer.

Cover photograph of New York City © Richard Berenholtz/The Stock Market

All rights reserved. No part of this book may be used or reproduced in any manner whatsoever without written permission except in the case of brief quotations embodied in critical articles or reviews. For information address St. Martin's Press, 175 Fifth Avenue, New York, NY 10010.

Library of Congress Catalog Card Number: 00-045994

ISBN: 0-312-98208-9

Printed in the United States of America

St. Martin's Press hardcover edition / March 2001
St. Martin's Paperbacks edition / February 2002

St. Martin's Paperbacks are published by St. Martin's Press, 175 Fifth Avenue, New York, NY 10010.

10 9 8 7 6 5 4 3 2

For my wife's retirement fund

Sometimes one wonders whether the
dragons of primeval ages are really extinct.

—SIGMUND FREUD

ON
A BEAM
OF
LIGHT

PROLOGUE

In March 1995, I published an account of sixteen sessions with a psychiatric patient who believed he came (on a beam of light) from a planet called K-PAX. The patient, a thirty-three-year-old male Caucasian who called himself "prot" (rhymes with "goat"), was, in fact, a double personality whose alter ego, Robert Porter, had been devastated by a severe emotional trauma. The latter survived only by hiding behind his formidable "alien" friend. When prot "returned" to his home planet at precisely 3:31 A.M. on August 17, 1990, promising to reappear "in about five of your years," Robert was left behind in a state of intractable catatonia, kept alive by constant monitoring and attentive care.

Many of the patients in residence at the Manhattan Psychiatric Institute at the time of prot's tenure have since departed. These include Chuck and Mrs. Archer (all names have been changed to protect individual privacy), who only recently moved out to a retirement complex on Long Island, thanks to an annuity established by her late husband; and Ed, a psychopath who gunned down six people in a shopping mall in 1986, but who has evinced little tendency toward violent behavior since a chance encounter with prot in 1990. He now lives in a community care home with La Belle Chatte, a former feline resident of MPI. The only patient mentioned in *K-PAX* who was still with us in 1995 was Russell, our resident "chaplain," who had nowhere else to go.

Nevertheless, all our inmates, even the most recent arrivals, were well aware of prot's promised return, and as the miserably hot, rainless summer days oozed by, the tension began to mount among patients and staff alike. (Only Klaus Villers, our director, remained unperturbed. In his opinion, "He vill neffer be back. Robert Porter vill be here foreffer.")

No one anticipated prot's return more than I, however, not only because of a paternal fondness I had developed for him during the course of our sessions together, but also because I still hoped to get Robert out of the catatonic ward and, with prot's help, on the long road to recovery.

But "about five years" from the time of prot's departure could have been anytime in 1995 or even later, so my wife and I went ahead with our usual plans to spend the middle two weeks of August at our Adirondack retreat.

That was a mistake. I was so preoccupied with the possibility of his imminent reappearance that I was very poor company for Karen and our friends, the Siegels, who tried every possible means to get my mind off my work. In hindsight I probably realized unconsciously that "five years" meant, to a mind as precise as prot's, sometime within minutes or hours of that exact interval. In fact, it was on Thursday, August 17, at 9:08 A.M., that I received a tearful call from Betty McAllister, our head nurse. "He's back!" was all she could say, and all she needed to.

"I'll be there this afternoon," I assured her. "Don't let him go anywhere!"

Karen (a psychiatric nurse herself) merely smiled, shook her head, and began to pack a lunch for my return trip to the city while I grabbed up unread reports and unfinished manuscripts and stuffed them into my briefcase.

The drive gave me a chance to reflect once more on the events of 1990, which I had reviewed only a few weeks earlier in preparation for his possible return. For the benefit of those who are not familiar with the history of the case, a brief summary follows:

Robert Porter was born and raised in Guelph, Montana. In 1975, when he was a high-school senior, he married a classmate, Sarah (Sally) Barnstable, who had become pregnant. The only job he could find to support his new wife and budding family was "knocking" steers in the local slaughterhouse, the same job that had killed his father some twelve years earlier.

One Saturday in August 1985, Robert arrived home from work to find a stranger coming out the front door. He chased the man through the house, past the bloody bodies of his wife and daughter, and into the backyard, where he broke the intruder's neck. Numb with grief, he attempted suicide by drowning in the nearby river. However, he washed ashore downstream, and from that moment forward was no longer Robert Porter, but "prot," a visitor

3

from the idyllic planet K-PAX, where all the terrible things that had befallen his alter ego could never happen.

Indeed, his was a truly utopian world, where everyone lived happily for a thousand years without the tiresome need to work for a living, where there was little or no sickness, poverty, or injustice, nor, for that matter, schools, governments, or religions of any kind. The only drawback to life on K-PAX seemed to be that sexual activity was so unpleasant that it was resorted to only to maintain the (low) population levels.

After prot, a true savant who knew a great deal about astronomical matters, was brought to MPI (how he got to New York is still a mystery), it took me several weeks to understand that he was a secondary personality behind whom his primary psyche was hiding and, with the help of Giselle Griffin, a freelance reporter, to identify that tragic soul as Robert Porter. But this revelation came too late. When prot "departed" the Earth on August 17, 1990, Robert, no longer able to hide behind his alter ego, retreated deep into the recesses of his own shattered mind.

Nothing, including a series of electroconvulsive treatments and the most powerful antidepressant drugs, had been of any use in arousing Robert from his rigor. I even tried hypnosis, which had proven so effective in revealing what had happened to him in 1985. He ignored me, as he did everyone else. Thus, it was with mounting excitement that I arrived at the hospital that hot August afternoon and hurried to his room, where I somehow expected prot to be ready and eager to get on with whatever he had "come back" to do. Instead, he was weak and unsteady, though a bit impatient to be up and going, as anyone who had spent five years in the fetal position would be. He was asking (more of a croak) for his favorite fruits, of course, and blamed his feeble state on his recent "voyage." Betty had already seen that he had some liquid nourishment, including a little apple juice, and Dr. Chakraborty, our chief internist, had ordered a sedative to help him sleep, which he did almost immediately after I arrived.

It may seem odd to the reader that prot needed rest after five years of inactivity, but the fact is that the catatonic patient, unlike the comatose, is neither asleep nor unconscious but rigidly awake, like a living statue, afraid to move for fear of committing further "reprehensible" acts. It is this muscle rigidity (sometimes alternating with frenetic activity) that results in the utter exhaustion the patient feels when he is finally aroused.

I decided to let him recuperate for a few days before bombarding him with the list of questions I had been compiling for half a decade and getting on with his (Robert's) treatment and, I fervently hoped, successful recovery.

Session Seventeen

I scheduled the first session (the seventeenth overall) with prot for 3:00 P.M., Monday, August 21, remembering to dim the lights for his sensitive eyes. Indeed, he removed his dark glasses as soon as he was escorted into my examining room by his old friend Roman Kowalski (Gunnar Jensen had retired), and I was delighted to find that he appeared to be fully recovered from five years of rigid immobility, though technically it was Robert, not prot, who had been catatonic throughout that period. He was, in fact, much as I remembered him: smiling, energetic, alert. The only notable changes were some weight loss and a hint of premature graying at the temples—he was now thirty-eight years old, though he claimed to be closer to four hundred.

Betty had reported that he was already able to eat soft, easily digestible foods, so I had a few overripe bananas on hand, which he dug into with his usual relish, skins and all. "The riper the better," he reminded me. "I like them pitch-black." He seemed utterly at home, as if our last session had been only yesterday.

I turned on the tape recorder. "How are you feeling, prot?" I asked him.

"A little tired, gene." Note to reader: prot capitalized the names of planets, stars, etc. Everything else, including human beings, was, to him, of little universal importance and therefore lowercase. "How about yourself?"

"Much better, now that you're back," I told him.

"Oh? Have you been ill?"

"Not exactly. Frustrated, mostly."

"Maybe you should see a psychiatrist."

"Actually, I've conferred with the best minds in the world about the source of my frustration."

"Does it have anything to do with your relationships with other humans?"

"In a way."

"I thought so."

"To be frank, it concerns you and Robert."

"Really? Have we done something wrong?"

"That's what I'd like to know. Maybe we could begin with your telling me where you've been for the past five years."

"Don't you remember, doc? I had to return to K-PAX for a while."

"And you took Bess with you?" Note: Bess was a psychotically depressed patient who "disappeared" in 1990 along with prot.

"I thought a change of scene would do her good."

"And where is she now?"

"Still on K-PAX."

"She didn't come back with you?"

"Nope."

"Why not?"

"Are you kidding? Would you want to come back to this place after you've seen pa-ree?" NB: the "place" he referred to was the Earth, not the hospital.

"Can you prove to me that Bess is on K-PAX?"

"Can you prove she is not?"

A familiar sinking feeling began to set in. "And how is she doing?"

"Like a fish in water. She laughs all the time now."

"And she didn't come back with you."

"Haven't we been over this?"

"What about all the other K-PAXians?"

"What about them?"

"Did anyone else come with you?"

"No. I wouldn't be surprised if no one ever did."

"Why not?"

"They read my report." He yawned. "Still, you never know. . . ."

"Tell me something: Why did you come to Earth in the first place, knowing from our radio and TV broadcasts that it was such an inhospitable planet?"

"I told you before: Robert needed me."

"That was in 1963?"

"By your calendar."

"Just in time for his father's funeral."

"In the nick."

"And you've made the trip several times since."

9

"Nine, to be exact."

"All right. Just for the record, then, you've been back on K-PAX for the past five years."

"Well, it's not that simple. There's the round trip, which—oh, I explained all that last time, didn't I? Let's just say I stayed around for a little r and r after turning in my report to the libraries. Then I hurried on back here."

"Why were you in such a hurry?"

"Ah, I get it. You're asking me questions you already know the answers to." There it was: the familiar Cheshire-cat grin. "Just for the record—right?"

"In your case, I don't know many of the answers yet, believe me."

"Oh, I can believe that, all right. But to answer your question: I promised certain beings I would come back in five of your years, remember?"

"To take them to K-PAX with you."

"Yep."

"So what's the rush?"

"They all seemed to want to leave as soon as possible."

"And how many of them do you plan to take back with you when you go?"

Up to this point prot had been gazing about the room as if searching for familiar objects, pausing occasionally to study the watercolors on the various walls. Now he looked directly into my eyes and his smile vanished. "I came prepared this time, doctor b. I can take as many as a hundred beings with me when I return."

"What? A *hundred*?"

"Sorry. Not enough room for more."

The transcript indicates a long pause before I could think

of a response. "Who do you think you'll be taking, for example?"

"Oh, I won't know that until the time comes."

I could feel my heart pounding as I asked, as casually as I could, "And when will that be?"

"Ah. That would be telling."

Now it was my turn to stare at him. "You mean you're not even going to tell me how long you'll be here?"

"I'm happy to see that your hearing is still unimpaired, narr" (pax-o for "gene," or "one who doubts").

"I'd really like to know that, prot. Can you give me some idea at least? Another five years? A month?"

"Sorry."

"Why the hell can't you tell me?"

"Because if you knew when I was leaving you'd watch me like a cat watches a bird in this carnivorous WORLD."

I had learned a long time ago that there was no use arguing with my "alien" friend. All I could do was make the best of whatever situation he sprang on me. "In that case, I'd like to schedule you for three weekly sessions. Every Monday, Wednesday, and Friday at three o'clock. Would that be all right with you?"

"Whatever you say, dahktah. For the time being I'm at your service."

"Good. There are a few more questions I'd like to ask you before you go back to your room."

He nodded sleepily.

"First, where did you land on this trip?"

"The pacific ocean."

"It was pointing toward K-PAX at the time?"

"Gino! You're finally getting it!"

"Tell me something. How do you breathe in outer space?"

He wagged his head. "I guess I spoke too soon. You still don't understand. The usual physical rules don't apply to light-travel."

"Well, what's it like? Are you awake? Do you feel anything?"

His fingertips came together and he frowned in concentration. "It's difficult to describe. Time seems to stand still. It's rather like a dream. . . ."

"And when you 'land'?"

"It's like waking up. Only you're somewhere else."

"It must be quite an awakening, finding yourself in the middle of an ocean. Can you swim?"

"Not a stroke. As soon as I bobbed up I got right out of there."

"How?"

He sighed. "I told you on my last visit, remember? It's done with mirrors. . . ."

"Oh. Right. And where else did you go before you came here?"

"Nowhere. Came straight home to mpi."

"Well, are you planning any excursions away from the hospital while you're here?"

"Not at the moment."

"If you do decide to take any side trips will you be sure to let me know?"

"Don't I always?"

"That reminds me—did Robert go with you on your trip to Labrador and Newfoundland the last time you were here?"

"Nope."

"Why not?"

"He didn't want to."

"We never saw him during the few days you were gone. Where was he?"

"No idea, coach. You'll have to ask *him*."

"Second: You're not planning any 'tasks' for the other patients (as he did for Howie, the violinist, five years ago), are you?"

"Gene, gene, gene. I just got here. I haven't even *met* any of the patients yet."

"But you'll tell me if you come up with any such plans?"

"Why not?"

"Good. And finally, are there any more little surprises you're not telling me about?"

"If I told you, they wouldn't be surprises, would they?"

I glared at him. "Prot—where is Robert?"

"Not far away."

"Have you spoken with him?"

"Of course."

"How is he feeling?"

"Like a sack of mot excrement." Note: A "mot" is a skunklike animal found on K-PAX.

"Did he say anything you'd like to tell me about?"

"He wanted to know what happened to the dog." He meant the dalmatian I had brought in, hoping to induce the catatonic Robert to respond to it.

"Tell him I took Oxeye home until he felt well enough to take care of him."

"Ah. Your famous carrot-and-stick routine."

"You could call it that. All right. This is my last question for today, but I want you to think about it before you answer."

He broke into another gigantic yawn.

"While you're here, will you help me make Robert feel better? Will you help him deal with his feelings of worthlessness and despair?"

"I'll do what I can. But you know how he is."

"Good. That's all anyone can do. Now—any objection to my trying hypnosis again during our next session?"

"You never give up, do you, doc?"

"We try not to." I stood up. "Thank you for coming in, prot. It's good to see you again." I went over and shook his hand. If he was still weak it didn't show in his handshake. "Shall I call Mr. Kowalski, or can you find your way back to your room?"

"It's not that difficult, gino."

"We'll move you back to Ward Two tomorrow."

"Good old ward two."

"See you Wednesday."

He threw me a backward wave as he shuffled out.

After prot had gone I listened, with mixed feelings of excitement and trepidation, to the tape of this brief session. Given enough time I was sure I could help Robert overcome the barriers blocking his recovery. But how much time would we have? In 1990 we were faced with a deadline that forced me to take chances, to hurry things too much. Now I was confronted with an even worse dilemma: I hadn't the slightest idea how long prot would be around.

The only clue I had was his passive response to my suggestion of thrice-weekly sessions. If he were planning to leave within a few days he would undoubtedly have responded with, "They'd better be productive!" or some such remark. But I could be wrong about that, as I have been about so many things where prot was concerned.

In any case three weekly sessions were all I could manage. Though I wouldn't be teaching during the fall term, there were other unavoidable responsibilities, not the least of which were my other patients, all difficult and puzzling cases, each deserving of my best efforts. One of these was a young woman I call Frankie (after the old song "Frankie and Johnny Were Lovers"), who is not only unable to love another human being but doesn't even understand the concept. Another was Bert, a loan officer at a bank, who spends all his waking hours searching for something he has lost, though he hasn't a clue as to what it is.

But back to prot. During the previous five years there had been ample opportunity to discuss his case with colleagues, both at MPI and around the world. There were no end of suggestions about how to deal with my problem patient. For example, one doctor from a former Soviet state assured me that Robert would be quickly cured by immersing him in ice water for several hours a day, a useless and inhumane practice that became obsolete decades ago. The consensus, however, was that hypnosis was still probably the best approach for Robert/prot, and I planned to begin essentially where I had left off in 1990. That is, to try to coax Robert out of his protective shell so I could help him deal with his devastating feelings about the tragic events of 1985.

In this effort I badly needed prot's help. Without it, I

felt the chances for recovery were slim. Thus, I was faced with another quandary: If Robert were to get well, prot would have to "dissolve" into, and become part of, his personality. How willing would he be to play a role in Robert's treatment and recovery if it came about at the expense of his own existence?

On Friday, the day after prot's return, I had called Giselle Griffin, the reporter who had been so instrumental in tracking down Robert's origins, to tell her he was back. She had come in regularly since prot's departure five years ago, ostensibly to check on Robert's progress, but secretly, I think, hoping to find that prot had returned, for she had fallen in love with him during the months she had spent at the hospital researching his story for *Conundrum* magazine. Of course she was often traveling far and wide, her most recent project (possibly anticipating prot's return) being an article on UFO's, which have been sighted almost everywhere. Nevertheless, she always left a beeper number and made it clear that she wanted to be informed of any change in Robert's condition.

She was very excited to hear about prot's reappearance and said she would be there "ASAP." I requested, however, that she not come to see him until he had recovered from his "journey" (i.e., the catatonia) and I had had a chance to speak with him, assuring her, perhaps erroneously, that there would be plenty of time to get reacquainted when he was stronger.

After the session with prot I phoned her again or, more accurately, left a message that she could call and set up an appointment to see him. After that I dictated a letter to Robert's mother in Hawaii, advising her that her son was no longer catatonic, but suggesting she also not visit until things were more certain. Then I toured the lower wards, intending to inform all the residents who were interested that prot was back, to pave the way for his return to Ward Two the following day.

The institute is structured so that the most seriously ill or dangerous patients occupy the top floors, while the least afflicted roam the first and second (Wards One and Two). Ward One, in fact, is primarily a temporary home for certain transient patients who come in periodically for a "tune-up," usually an adjustment in their medication, and for those who have made substantial progress toward recovery and are nearly ready for discharge. Prot was about to rejoin the inhabitants of Two, patients suffering serious psychoses ranging from manic depression to acute obsessive-compulsive disorder, but who are not a menace to the staff or each other.

I needn't have bothered. It was obvious from the moment I entered the ward that everyone already knew about prot's return. A psychiatric hospital is similar to a small town in some ways—news travels fast, and moods seem almost communicable. On this, the day before prot was to take up residence among them, the atmosphere was virtually electric with anticipation. Even some of the severe depressives greeted me relatively cheerfully, and a chronic schizophrenic, who hadn't uttered an intelligible sentence in months, inquired, I believe, after my health. And most of these patients, except for Russell and a few others, had never even met him.

Giselle showed up at my office on Tuesday morning, sans appointment, as I expected. I had not seen her for several weeks, but I had not forgotten her piney fragrance, the doelike eyes.

She was dressed, as always, in an old shirt, faded jeans, and running shoes with no socks. Though pushing forty, she still looked like a kid—a sixteen-year-old girl with crow's-feet. Yet, there was something different about her. She was not so ebullient as she was five years ago. Gone was the coy smile I had once mistaken for coquettishness but which I had learned was a part of her truly ingenuous nature. Instead, she seemed uncharacteristically nervous. It occurred to me that she might be apprehensive about meeting prot again, distressed, I supposed, that he might have changed, or perhaps had even forgotten her.

"Don't worry," I reassured her. "He's exactly the same."

She nodded, but the distant look in those big brown eyes suggested she hadn't heard me.

"Tell me what you've been up to the last couple of months."

Her eyes suddenly came into focus. "Oh. I'm almost finished with the piece on UFO's. That's why I haven't been around for a while."

"Good. Are they real or—"

"Depends on who you talk to."

"What if you talked to yourself?"

"I'd say no. But there are plenty of sane, normal people who would disagree."

"Yet you believe that prot came from K-PAX."

"Yes, but he didn't come in a UFO."

"Ah." I waited, which seemed to make her nervous again.

"Dr. Brewer?"

I was pretty sure I knew what was coming. "Yes, Giselle?"

"I'd like to come back to the hospital for a while. I want to find out what he really knows."

"About UFO's?"

"About everything. I want to write a book about it."

"Giselle, you know a psychiatric hospital isn't grist for the public mill. The only reason I let you work here the last time is that you performed a valuable service for us."

"But I would be performing another valuable service this time, one that might benefit *everyone*." She curled up in the black vinyl chair across from my desk. "You're probably going to write another book about him as a patient, right? Mine will be different. I want to find out everything he knows, catalog it, check it all out, and see what the world can learn from his knowledge. Which you'll have to admit is pretty remarkable, whether you believe he comes from K-PAX or not." She bowed her head for a moment, then looked up at me with those pleading doe eyes. "I won't be in the way, I promise."

I wasn't convinced of that. But I wasn't so sure her proposal was such a bad idea, either. I knew she could be of considerable help in my dealings with prot (and later, perhaps, with Robert). "I'll tell you what. You can do it under two conditions."

She abruptly uncoiled and sat facing me like a puppy waiting for a treat.

"First, you can only interview him for an hour a day. Despite your feelings about prot, he's not here to help you write a book."

She nodded.

"And second, you'll have to have his consent. If he isn't interested in cooperating with you, that's the end of it."

"I agree. But if he doesn't like the idea, I can still visit him, can't I?"

"During regular visiting hours and under the usual conditions."

She knew, of course, that our rules were liberal, and she could talk with him most evenings and on weekends (inasmuch as reporters and curiosity seekers were screened out, it was unlikely that he would have many other visitors). "Done!" She jumped up and extended a tiny hand, which I took. "Now can I see him?"

"One more thing," I added as we headed (Giselle skipped) for Ward Two. "See if you can find out when he's leaving."

Her face fell. "He's leaving?"

"Don't worry—it won't be for a while. And when he does, he's going to take a few people back with him."

"He is? Who?"

"That's what I'd like you to find out."

When we got to Two, we found prot in the lounge surrounded by several of the other patients, all of whom seemed to be talking at once. The ward's half-dozen cats were competing for space to rub against his legs. Rudolph, the self-proclaimed "greatest dancer in the universe," was pirouetting around the room. Russell was running back and forth crying, "Praise the Lord! The Teacher is at hand!"

Milton, our peripatetic jokester, shouted, "Chairs for the standing army!" Others were mumbling incomprehensibly, and I made a mental note to ask prot later whether he could understand any of their parlance. There were presents, too: peanut butter and fruit (known from his previous visit to be favorites of his), and the gossamer thread, an invisible talisman left on the lawn one drizzly day five years earlier by "the bluebird of happiness."

When he saw Giselle he broke away from the group and approached her with arms outstretched. He hugged her warmly and then stepped back and gazed silently into her eyes. Prot obviously remembered her, and fondly.

Having other duties to perform, I left them alone and hurried to meet with my first patient of the day.

When I got to my examining room I found that Messrs. Rodrigo and Kowalski were waiting outside with Michael, a twenty-two-year-old male Caucasian who had tried to kill himself on at least three occasions before coming to MPI.

He's not the only one. Suicide rates in the United States, and many other countries, have increased dramatically over the past several years, particularly among the young, and nobody seems to have a good explanation for this tragic phenomenon. There are many reasons why a person might try to take his own life—grief, stress, general depression, failure of one's expectations, feelings of hopelessness—but none of these in itself is the root cause of a suicidal tendency (most grieving and depressed people do not attempt to end their lives). As with all medical problems, each case has to be treated individually. The therapist must try to determine the reason for the patient's self-destructive feelings and help him deal with them by proposing more reasonable solutions to the problems causing his suffering.

Michael, for example, holds himself responsible for the death of his identical twin brother, and desperately wants to "even the score." Although it's true that he was instrumental in initiating the events that led to his twin's demise, it was an accident that could have befallen anyone. I have not been able to convince him of this, however, nor to absolve him of his deep feelings of responsibility and guilt ("Why him, not me?").

But Mike takes this logic one step farther than most. He feels himself responsible for the fate of everybody whose path he has ever crossed, afraid he might have started a chain reaction of catastrophic events. Ordinarily he keeps his distance from me and everyone else, avoiding eye contact, saying little.

Not this time. Though unkempt and sloppily dressed, as usual, he came into the room in good spirits (for him). He even tried to smile. I remarked upon this, hoping there had been a genuine change in his attitude toward life. And there was. He had heard about prot, and was eagerly waiting to meet him. "Don't worry," he added, looking me right in the eye, "I'm not going to make another attempt until I talk to the guy from K-PAX." When I looked dubious he actually grinned and raised a scarred arm in salute. "Scout's honor."

There's an old axiom in psychiatry: "Beware of the cheerful suicidal." I knew he was serious and probably would wait to hear what prot's solution to his problems might be.

But I certainly wouldn't decrease his surveillance, nor move him down from Three.

As I mused about what prot could possibly do for Michael, and perhaps some of the others, I suddenly realized that his return presented us with another dilemma. All the inmates had heard about prot's earlier visit and hopes were running high, perhaps much too high, that he would be able to chase away all the dragons breathing fire down their necks, as he had done with many of our former patients. I couldn't help wondering: What would happen to a patient like Michael, whose last hopes would be dashed if prot failed to meet those rosy expectations?

That afternoon I cleaned off my desk, or tried to—when I was finished it looked as crowded as before—and found a paper awaiting my review, which had been due two weeks earlier. I started to read it but all I could think of was my next session with prot. Although he had only just returned, I already felt exhausted. It's at times like this that I contemplate with great seriousness an early retirement, a bug my wife keeps flicking into my ear.

Many people have the following idea about psychiatrists, and perhaps about physicians in general: We work whenever we wish, take long weekends, spend a lot of time on vacation. And even when we do come to the office we don't do any real work and for this we command enormous fees. It isn't like that, believe me. It's a twenty-four-hour-a-day job. Even when we aren't attending to our patients or on call we're running case histories through our minds, trying to think of something we might have forgotten that would help a suffering individual. And the stress of making a mistake takes its toll as well. We often sleep poorly, eat too much, don't get enough exercise—all the things we preach against.

I ended up reviewing prot's entire file again, unfortunately without any new ideas coming to mind. And I knew I wouldn't get much sleep that night or any other until Robert came forth and, together, we exorcised the demons roaring thunderously in the recesses of his tormented mind.

SESSION EIGHTEEN

On the morning of prot's next session I got a call from Charlie Flynn, the astronomer from Princeton and my son-in-law Steve's colleague, who was studying the planetary system prot claimed to have come from. His voice reminded me of a squeaky wheel. "Why didn't you tell me he was back?" he demanded, without even a "Hello."

"I—"

"Whoa. You have to understand that prot is a patient of mine. He's not here for your benefit, nor anyone else's."

"I disagree."

"That's not for you to decide!" I snapped. I hadn't slept well the night before.

"Who does decide such matters? There is a great deal he can tell us. The things we've learned from him already have changed our way of thinking about certain astronomical problems, and I'm sure we've only scratched the surface. We need him."

"My first responsibility is to my patient, not the world of astronomy."

There was a brief pause while he reconsidered his approach. "Of course. Of course. Look. I'm not asking you to sacrifice him on the altar of science. All I'm asking is that you let us talk with him when he's not undergoing therapy or whatever."

I could understand his position and, indeed, the refrain was beginning to sound familiar. "I'll offer you a compromise," I told him.

"Oh, no. Submitting a list of questions like last time just won't do it."

"If I let you talk to him directly, then every astronomer in the country is going to be banging on the door."

"But I banged first."

"No you didn't. Someone got here before you did."

"What? Who?"

"The reporter who helped us fill in his background five years ago. Giselle Griffin."

"Oh. Her. But what has she got to do with this? She's not a scientist, is she?"

"Nevertheless, here's my proposal. You and everyone else can talk to him through her. Is that acceptable?"

Another pause. "I'll make you a counteroffer. I'll agree to your proposition if I can speak directly with him just once. We were in on this thing five years ago, too, and we helped identify him as a true savant, remember?"

"Okay, but you'll have to work it out with her. She has him for an hour a day."

"How do I reach her?"

"I'll ask her to contact you."

After grumbling something about reporters, he hung up. I immediately called the head of our secretarial pool to request that she direct all requests for information about prot to Giselle.

"Does that include the stack of mail we've gotten over the past few years?"

"Everything," I told her, eager to get this can of worms out of my hair.

When Giselle's article featuring prot came out in 1992, it precipitated a flurry of calls and letters to the hospital. Most were requests for information about prot's home planet and directions on how to get there. When *K-PAX* appeared three years later, several thousand more queries came in from all over the world. A lot of people, it seemed, wanted to find some way, short of suicide, to get off the planet. Since we had no answers to these questions, most of the correspondence was filed away without response.

On the other hand, all the requests for copies of his "report," an assessment of life on Earth and his dim prognosis for the future of Homo sapiens, have been honored. This treatise, "Preliminary Observations on B-TIK (RX 4987165.233)," has generated a certain amount of controversy among scientists, many of whom believe that his prediction of our imminent demise is greatly exaggerated, that only a crazy person would call for an end to established social customs, which, in prot's eyes, fuel the fire of our self-immolation.

As for myself, I take prot's report, and all his other observations and pronouncements, for what they are—the utterances of a remarkable man who may be able to utilize part(s) of his brain unavailable to the rest of us, except, perhaps, for those suffering from other forms of savant syndrome. In prot's case, however, a substantial portion of his brain belonged to someone else: his alter ego, Robert Porter. It was Robert, a desperately ill patient, whom I so badly needed and wanted to help, even if it came at prot's expense.

"Peaches!" prot exclaimed as he strode into my examining room. He was wearing his favorite attire: sky-blue denim shirt and matching corduroy pants. "I haven't had one of these in years! *Your* years, that is." He offered me a taste and then opened wide to bite into a ripe one himself. A jet of saliva squirted halfway across the room.

This was one of the few fruits whose seeds he did not consume. I asked him why.

"Hard on the teeth," he explained, clanking one of the pits back into the bowl. "Dentist fodder."

"You have dentists on K-PAX?"

"Heaven forbid."

"Lucky you."

"Luck has nothing to do with it."

"While you're eating, let me just ask you: Are you planning to write another report on us?"

"Nope," he replied with a great slurp. "Not unless there have been some major changes since my last visit." He paused and gave me his sincere, innocent look. "There haven't been, have there?"

"You mean on Earth."

"That's where we are, ain't it?"

"Not that you would call major, I suppose."

"I was afraid of that."

"No world wars, though," I said brightly.

"Just the usual dozens of regional ones."

"But that's progress, don't you think?"

He grinned at this, though it looked more like an animal baring its teeth. "That's one of the funniest things about this place. You kill millions and millions of beings every day, and if you murder a few less on the next one, you nearly break your arms patting yourselves on the back. On K-PAX you humans are a riot."

"C'mon, prot, we don't kill 'millions and millions' of people every day."

"I didn't say 'people.' " Another pit rang into the bowl like the peal of a cheerful bell.

I had forgotten that he considered all animals equally important, even insects. I decided to change the subject. "Have you spoken with any of the other patients since I last saw you?"

"They have spoken to me, mostly."

"I suppose they all want to go back with you."

"Not all of them."

"Tell me: Are you able to communicate with everyone in Ward Two?"

"Of course. So could you if you tried."

"Even the ones who don't speak?"

"They all speak. You just have to learn how to listen."

I have long believed that if we could understand what certain unintelligible patients were saying, i.e., how their thoughts differed from normal, we could learn a lot about the nature of their afflictions. "What about the schizo-phrenics? I mean the ones whose words seem garbled—can you understand what they're saying?"

"Certainly."

"How do you do that?"

Prot threw up his hands. "You remember the tape you played for me five years ago? The one of the whale songs?"

"Yes."

"What a memory! Well, there you are."

"I don't—"

"You've got to stop treating your patients as if they were carbon copies of yourself. If you were to treat them as be-ings from whom you might learn something, you would."

"Can you help me do that?"

"I could, but I won't."

"Why not?"

"You have to learn it for yourself. You'd be surprised how easy it is if you forget everything you've been taught and start over."

"Are you talking about my patients, or the Earth again?"

"It's the same thing, wouldn't you say?" He pushed the bowl of pits away and sat gazing contentedly toward the ceiling, as if he hadn't a care in the world.

"What about Robert?" I asked.

"What about him?"

"Have you spoken to him in the last day or so?"

"He's still not saying much. But . . ."

"But—what?"

"I have the feeling he's ready to cooperate with you."

I sat up straighter. "He is? How do you know? What did he say?"

"He didn't say anything. It's just a feeling I have. He seems—I don't know—a little tired of hiding. Of everything."

"Everything? He's not planning to—"

"Nah. He's just tired of being tired, I think."

"I'm very glad to hear that."

"I suppose that's what you would call 'progress.'"

I stared at him for a moment, wondering whether Robert might be willing to come out even without hypnosis.

"He's not *that* tired, gene," prot remarked.

I could feel my shoulders slumping. "In that case, we'll begin now. If you're ready."

"Whenever you are."

"Good. Do you remember the little spot on the wall behind me?"

"Of course. One-two-three-four-five." And he was out like a light.

"Prot?"

"Yes, dr. b?"

"How do you feel?"

"A little spacey."

"Very funny. Now—do you remember what happened the last time I spoke with you in this setting?"

"Certainly. It was a hot day and you were sweating a lot."

"That's right. And Robert wouldn't speak to me—remember?"

"Of course."

"Will he speak to me now?"

There was a pause before prot abruptly slouched down in his chair.

"Robert?"

No response.

"Robert, the last time I spoke with you was under very different circumstances. I didn't know much about you then. Since that time I have learned why you are suffering so much, and I want to try to help you cope with that. I'm not going to make any promises this time. It won't be easy, and you'll have to help me. For now, I only want to chat with you, get to know you better. Do you understand? Let's just talk about the happy times in your life or anything else you'd like to discuss. Will you talk to me now?"

He made no response.

"I want you to consider this room a safe haven. This is a place where you can say anything that's on your mind without fear or guilt or shame, and nothing will happen to you or to anyone else. Please remember that."

No response.

"I'll tell you what. I've got some information here on your background. I'm going to read it to you, and you stop me if I say anything that's incorrect. Will you do that?"

Again there was no response, but I thought I detected a slight tilt of Robert's head, as if he wanted to hear what I had to say.

"All right. You were a star wrestler in high school with an overall record of 26-8. You were captain of the team and finished second in the state tournament your senior year."

Robert said nothing.

"You were a good student and won a scholarship to the state university. You were also awarded a community-service medal by the Guelph Rotary Club in 1974. You were vice president of your class for three years running. All right so far?"

Still no response.

"You and your wife Sarah and your daughter Rebecca lived in a trailer for the first seven years of your marriage, and then you built a house in the country near a forest with a stream. It sounds like a beautiful place. The kind of place I'd like to retire to someday. . . ."

I glanced at Robert and, to my surprise, found him staring at me. I didn't ask him how he felt. He looked terrible. "I'm sorry," he croaked.

I wasn't clear what he was sorry about—it could have been any number of things. But I said, immediately, "Thank you, Robert. I'm sorry, too."

His eyes slammed shut and his head dropped down again. Apparently the only reason he had come out was to offer this pathetic apology to me, or perhaps to the world. I gazed at him sadly for a moment before he sat up and stretched.

"Thank you, prot."

"For what?"

"For—never mind. All right, I'm going to wake you up now. I'm going to count back from five to one. You will awaken slowly, and when I get to—"

"Five-four-three-two-one," he sang out. "Hiya, doc. Did Rob say anything to you yet?" Note: When awake, prot could not remember anything that transpired while he was under hypnosis.

"Yes, he did."

"No kidding? Well, it was only a matter of time."

33

"The question is, how much time do we have?"

"All the time in the WORLD."

"Prot, do you know anything about Rob that I don't know?"

"Such as?"

"Why he feels so worthless?"

"No idea, coach. Probably has something to do with his life on EARTH."

"But you talk to him, don't you?"

"Not about that."

"Why not?"

"He doesn't want to."

"Maybe he does now."

"Don't hold your breath."

"Okay, I'll let you off the hook for today. See if you can find out anything more from Robert, and I'll see you again on Friday."

"Put plenty of fruit on that hook," he advised as he ambled out.

I was on the "back forty" watching a badminton game played without shuttlecocks when Giselle came running toward me. I hadn't seen her since her encounter with prot two days earlier. "It's like you said," she panted. "He's just the same!"

I asked her whether he had told her when he was leaving.

"Not yet," she confessed. "But he doesn't seem to be in any hurry!" She looked absolutely moonstruck.

I reminded her to try to find out when it would be and

to let me know "ASAP." "But be subtle about it," I added inanely.

It didn't surprise me to learn that she had already gone through all the correspondence the hospital had received about prot and K-PAX. What did, however, was the information that more letters were beginning to come in.

"But nobody knows he's back."

"Somebody does! Or maybe they just anticipated his return. But the amazing thing is that a lot of them were addressed specifically to prot, care of MPI, or to prot, K-PAX. Or to the hospital with the notation to 'please forward.' In fact, some were just addressed to 'prot,' no address given."

"So I heard."

"But don't you see what that means?"

"What?"

"It means that a lot of people wanted their letters or calls to go directly to prot, not to anyone else."

"Isn't that what you would expect?"

"Not really. Furthermore, a lot of it was marked PERSONAL AND CONFIDENTIAL."

"So?"

"So I think most people don't trust us with the letters. I wouldn't, would you?"

Perhaps she was right. I had read some of those addressed to me, many of which began: "You idiot!"

While I was mulling over this unwanted development, she added, "Besides, you may have a legal problem if you don't turn them over to him."

"What legal problem?"

"Tampering with the U.S. mails."

"Don't be ridiculous. Prot is a patient here, and we have a right—"

"Maybe you should ask your lawyer."

"Maybe I will."

"No need. I already spoke to him. There was a case in 1989 in which evidence obtained from the correspondence of a patient at one of the state institutions was thrown out of court as illegal search and seizure. On top of that the hospital was fined for tampering with the mails. Anyway," she argued further, "if he's just a part of Robert's personality as you seem to think, what harm can it possibly do?"

"I don't know," I answered truthfully, thinking more about Robert than about a stack of Santa Claus mail or what prot might do with it. "All right. But just give him the ones specifically addressed to him." I suddenly felt like a Watergate criminal trying to minimize the damage, though I didn't know what the fallout might be.

"Next item. I got a call from Dr. Flynn last night."

"Oh, yes. I was going to ask you to call him."

"I guess he couldn't wait. Anyway, I arranged for him to meet with prot."

"Just don't let him take too much of prot's time. He won't be the last caller you'll have."

"I know. I've already heard from a cetologist and an anthropologist."

"Maybe that's enough for now. . . ."

"We'll see." She skipped away, leaving me alone with Jackie, a thirty-two-year-old "child," who was sitting on the damp ground (the lawn had been watered during the lunch hour) near the outer wall, digging a hole and ecstatically smelling each spoonful of the soft earth before squeezing it into a ball and carefully stacking it on top of the others. She had a mustache of soil, but I wasn't about to stop her and suggest she wash her dirty face.

Like many of our patients, Jackie has a tragic history. She was raised on a sheep farm in Vermont and spent most of her time out-of-doors. Home-schooled and isolated from close contact with other children, she developed an early interest in nature in all its color and variety. Unfortunately, Jackie's parents were killed in an automobile accident when she was nine, and she was compelled to live with an aunt in Brooklyn. Almost immediately after that, on the playground of her new school, she was accidentally shot in the stomach by a ten-year-old boy trying to avenge the murder of an older brother. When she came out of the hospital she was mute, and she hasn't spoken a word, nor mentally aged a day, since that time. In fact, one of the nurses still puts her hair up in pigtails, as her mother used to do when she was a girl.

Though she suffered no brain damage, nothing we have tried has proven successful in bringing her out of her dream world, the childhood she loved so much. She appears to live in a hypnotic state of her own making, from which we cannot arouse her.

But how she enjoys that world! When she plays with a toy or one of the cats she throws her entire being into it, focusing her concentration to the point of ignoring all outside stimuli, much like our autists. She takes in a sunset, or the sparrows flocking in the ginkgo trees, with rapture and serenity. It is a pleasure to watch her eat, her eyes closed and her mouth making little smacking noises.

It was patients like Jackie, and Michael, and others at

the hospital that I vaguely hoped prot, before he disappeared again, might be able to help. God knows we weren't doing much for them. Already he was instrumental in getting Robert to come out for a moment, if only to say he was sorry. But about what? Perhaps that he wasn't going to be able to go through with it, to cooperate in his treatment. Or maybe it was, in fact, what it appeared to be: a hopeful sign, an attempt to communicate, a small beginning.

That afternoon, as I was hurrying to get to a committee meeting, I spotted prot in the rec room talking with two of our most pathetic patients. One of these is a twenty-seven-year-old Mexican-American male who is obsessed with the notion that he can fly if he simply puts his mind to it. His favorite author, of course, is Gabriel García Márquez. No amount of medication or psychotherapy can convince him that only birds, bats, and insects can take to the air, and he spends most of his waking hours flapping back and forth across the lawn, never rising more than a foot or two above the ground.

How did this sorry condition come about? Manuel was the fourteenth of fourteen children. As such, he was the last into the bathtub, never got his share of the limited food, never had any new clothes, not even underwear or socks. On top of that, he was the "runt" of the bunch, barely making five feet in height. As a result he grew up with almost no self-esteem, and considered himself a failure before his life had even begun.

For reasons known only to himself he set an impossible

goal: to fly. If he could accomplish this, he decided, he would be fit to join the ranks of his fellow human beings despite all his other "failures." He has been at it since he was sixteen.

The other is an African-American homosexual—I'll call him Lou—who firmly believes he is pregnant. What makes him think so? If he places his hand on his abdomen he can feel the baby's pulse. Arthur Beamish (who is gay himself), his staff physician and our newest psychiatrist, has not been able to convince him that *everyone's* abdomen pulses with the beat of the abdominal aorta and other arteries, or to persuade him that fertilization in a man is impossible due to the absence of a major component of the reproductive system, namely an egg cell.

What has led to this bizarre conception? Lou has the mind of a woman trapped in a man's body, a not uncommon gender-identity problem known as transsexualism. When he was a child he enjoyed dressing in his big sister's clothing. His unmarried mother, who had problems of her own, encouraged this practice and insisted he urinate sitting down, and it wasn't until he was twelve years old that the truth was discovered during a routine school physical. By that time Lou's sexuality was firmly established in his mind. Indeed, he refers to himself as "she," something the staff does not encourage as it would only make things worse. Oddly, a benign cyst in his bladder caused some occasional minor bleeding, a fact he used to "prove," at least to himself, that he was menstruating.

Although a subject of intense verbal abuse throughout high school, he stubbornly maintained his female characteristics, wearing skirts and bras, using makeup, etc. He padded his breasts, of course, but so did some of the girls. After graduation, he and his mother moved to a different state where no one knew them, and Lou's identity was secure. He got a job as a secretary for a large corporation, and it wasn't long afterward that he fell in love with a man who happened to notice his five o'clock shadow in the elevator late one afternoon. A passionate relationship followed, and it was only a few months later that the urinary bleeding mysteriously stopped and Lou took this to mean he was pregnant. He was ecstatic. He badly wanted to have a child in order to validate his existence. Almost immediately thereafter he was afflicted with morning sickness, abdominal pains, fatigue, and all the rest. He has been wearing maternity clothes ever since.

The "father" of his child, frightened by something he did not understand, convinced Lou to seek psychiatric help, and he ended up with us at MPI. That was six months ago, and the baby is "due" in a few weeks. What will happen when it comes to term is a matter of conjecture and concern among staff members and patients alike. Lou, however, awaits that fateful day with sublime anticipation, as do some of the other inmates, who are already suggesting possible names for the new arrival.

SESSION NINETEEN

I think I found the focus for my book," Giselle announced as I was coming out of my office.

"I'm on my way to a meeting. Want to walk?"

"Sure." She fell in beside me with quick little steps.

"Isn't it space travel? UFO's? Little green men?"

"Not really. The first chapter will be about the likelihood of extraterrestrial life. The second will be a rehash of my article about UFO's. It's the other chapters I'm talking about."

"Have you asked him about UFO's?"

"Uh-huh."

"Well, what does he think?"

"He says 'There ain't any.' "

"How does he know that?"

"He says it would be like riding a pogo stick a trillion times around the Earth."

"So how does he account for all the sightings that people claim?"

"Wishful thinking."

"Huh?"

"He says that even though there are no alien ships, there are a lot of humans who would like to believe otherwise."

Klaus Villers joined us. "Hi, Klaus. What's the focus of the other chapters, Giselle?"

"Whether or not he has any special powers. If he has *one*, maybe there are others."

"You mean can he travel at superlight speed? That sort of thing?"

"Exactly. But there are other things, too."

"Such as?"

"Well, we both know he can talk to animals, right?"

"Hold on. *He* says he can talk to animals, but how do we know that?"

"Has he ever lied to you?"

"That's not the point. He may *believe* he can talk to them but that's not the same as fact. Nor is anything else he says that we can't verify."

"*I* believe him."

"That's your prerogative."

"Anyway, I'm going to try to find out whether he can or not. If he can, maybe he's telling the truth about everything else."

"Maybe and maybe not. But how do you propose to find out?"

"I'm going to ask him to speak with some animals whose history we know something about, and to tell me what they said to him."

"Well, all we have are the cats."

"That's a start. But they all came from a pound, and we know very little about them. And cats never say much anyway. I've got a better idea."

We stopped at the amphitheater. "This is where we get off." I thought Klaus would go on in, but he stopped, too. I glanced at my watch. "So what's your idea?"

"I want to take him to the zoo."

"Giselle! You know we can't let you take prot to the zoo. Or anywhere else."

"No, I mean make it an outing for all the patients in Wards One and Two. Or any others you think might want to go along." I heard Villers grunt. Whether it was a positive or a negative response, I couldn't tell.

"Look, we've got to get to this meeting. Let me think about it."

"Okay, boss. But you *know* it's a good idea." And off she went, half walking, half running, presumably to find prot. Villers stared after her.

I didn't pay much attention at the executive committee meeting, which had to do with ways to trim the budget in the wake of government cutbacks for treatment and research. I was thinking about prot's alleged "superhuman" abilities. What had he really done that was so amazing? True, he knew a lot about astronomy, but so did Dr. Flynn and many others. He somehow managed to get from his room to Bess's under our very noses five years ago. But that could have been some kind of hypnotic trick or simple inattention on our part. The only really inexplicable talent he possessed was his ability to "see" UV light, but even that had not been rigorously tested. None of these "powers" required an extraterrestrial origin. In any case, my chief concern was with Robert, and not prot.

When the budget meeting was over Klaus stopped me in the hall. "Ve should get a cut of her book," he whispered.

Owing to prot's influence, perhaps, I decided to have lunch in Ward Two. Betty and a couple of the other nurses joined us.

Everyone waited until I sat down. Prot took his place at the end of the table and all eyes were on him as he dug into his vegetables. He refused to eat any of the hot dogs, of course, as did some of his closest followers. He also declined the lime gelatin, saying he could "smell the flesh" in it. Frankie, who was already considerably overweight, eagerly relieved them of the leftovers, gobbling them down to the accompaniment of various bodily noises.

I glanced around the table at these unfortunate souls, some of whom had been here most of their lives, and tried to imagine what their worlds must be like. Russell, for example, though much improved from his Christ-like delusions of five years ago, was still unable to engage in normal conversation, preferring instead to quote endless passages from the Bible. I couldn't begin to get inside his head and imagine a life so limited, so joyless.

And Bert. What a frustrating existence, an eternity of worry and sorrow. What was it about his brain that precluded his dealing with his undeterminable loss and moving on? Whatever it was, his easy solution to all his problems, like that of almost everyone else present, was a trip to K-PAX, where difficulties like his didn't exist. In fact, Betty told me before lunch that the patients couldn't hear enough about the place. "It's like Lenny and the rabbits," she said. (Betty has read all of Steinbeck's novels more than once.)

When we had finished eating, Milton stood up and rapped on the table. "Went to the doctor the other day," he quipped. Some of the others were already tittering. "Told him I wanted somebody who knew what he was doing. He puffed out his chest and said, 'I've been practicing medicine for more than thirty years.' I said, 'I'll come back when you've got it right!' " Everyone was looking at me, giggling, waiting for my reaction. What else could I do but laugh, too?

I was still thinking about possible strategies to get Robert to stay around for a while when prot marched in for our nineteenth session. "Why didn't you tell me about the letters?" he inquired impishly as he reached for the fruit bowl.

"I was going to," I replied. "As soon as I thought you were ready to deal with them."

"Very interesting," he replied, biting into a persimmon.

"What—the letters?"

The fruit made his mouth pucker up. "Don't you find it amazing that so many beings want to get off this PLANET? Doesn't that tell you something?"

"It tells me we have our problems. But after all, the Earth has a population of six billion people, and only a few thousand called or wrote to you." I remember feeling quite smug about this rejoinder.

"Very likely because those are the only beings who read your book or Giselle's article. Hardly anyone on your

WORLD reads much, if at all." He finished the persimmon and reached for another. "We don't have anything like this on K-PAX. You should see what they look like in UV light!" He smacked his lips loudly and gazed thoughtfully at the fruit.

"Do you plan to answer them?"

"The persimmons?"

"No, dammit. The letters."

"I'll try. Most will be condolences, of course. I can only take a hundred beings with me when I go back, remember?"

"How many have you lined up so far?"

"Now, gene, if I gave you an obon, you'd take a jart."

"So you won't tell me. Nor will you tell me when you'll be leaving. I must confess, prot, I'm very disappointed that you still don't trust me."

"As long as we're being so honest and direct, doctor b, perhaps you could explain to me why human beings take everything so personally."

"I'll tell you what: I'll answer that if you'll tell me how long you're going to stay around."

"No way. But don't worry—I won't be leaving for a while yet. I've got the letters to consider and a few other things to take care of. . . ." He swallowed the last of the fruit and sat back, still smacking his lips. "Ready, doc?"

Sometimes I felt as though I were the patient and prot the doctor. "Just about. I'd like to speak to Robert first."

Without a word his eyes closed and his head slumped to his chest.

"Robert?"

No response.

"Robert, can you hear me?"

If he could, he didn't let on. There was no need to waste any more time. Obviously he still wasn't ready to cooperate, at least not without hypnosis. "All right, prot, you can come back out now."

"My tongue feels like cotton," he declared.

"That's the persimmons. Okay, I think we're ready now."

He gazed at the little white dot on the wall behind me. "Weird fruit. One-two-three-four—"

I waited until I was sure he was in a trance. "You may leave your eyes closed for a while, prot."

"Whatever you say, gino."

"Good. Now I'd like Robert to come forward, please. Rob? Can you hear me?"

His head dropped again.

"Robert, if you can hear me, please nod."

He nodded almost imperceptibly.

"Thank you. How are you feeling?"

"Not very good," he mumbled.

"I'm sorry. I hope I can help you feel better soon. Please listen to me and trust me. Remember, this is your safe haven."

No response.

"I thought we might talk a little about your childhood today. Your family. About growing up in Montana. Would that be all right?"

A feeble shrug.

"Good. Will you open your eyes, please?"

They blinked open, but he avoided my gaze.

"Why don't you tell me something about your mother."

Softly but clearly: "What do you want to know?"

47

"Anything you'd like to tell me. Is she a good cook?"

He seemed to consider the question carefully, or maybe he was simply trying to decide whether to respond. "Pretty good," he said.

I couldn't help feeling excited about this simple answer. It came in a lifeless monotone, but it represented a tremendous breakthrough, something I was afraid might take weeks of persistent cajoling. Robert was talking!

The remainder of the session proceeded rather haltingly, but he seemed to become more at ease as we chatted about some of the basic elements of his childhood: his sisters, his friends, his early school years and favorite activities—books and puzzles and watching the animals in the fields behind the house. His pre-adolescent boyhood seemed to be a perfectly normal one, unusual only in that he lost his father when he was six (at which time prot made his first appearance), though I didn't bring that up in this session. I merely wanted to gain Robert's confidence, make him feel comfortable talking with me. The real work would come later.

The discussion ended with Robert's telling me about a memorable day he had spent, when he was nine, roaming the fields with Apple, his big, shaggy dog, and I hoped that finishing on this happy note might encourage him to come forward less reluctantly the next time. But before I recalled prot I tried something I was pretty sure wouldn't work. I reached over, picked up a tiny whistle I had brought in for the occasion, and blew it loudly. "Do you hear that?"

"Yes."

"Good. Whenever you hear that sound I want you to

come forward, no matter where you are or what you are doing. Do you understand?"

"Yes."

"Good. Now I'd like to speak with prot, if you don't mind. Thanks for coming, Robert, and I'll see you later. Please close your eyes."

They drooped shut.

I waited a moment. "Prot? Please open your eyes."

"Hiya, gene. What's up?"

"The opposite of down?"

"Dr. brewer! You *do* have a sense of humor!"

"Thanks a lot. Now just relax. I'm going to count back from fi—"

"Five-four-three-two—Hey! Are we finished already?"

"Yes, we are. How did you know?"

"Just a feeling I get sometimes. Like I've missed something."

"I know how it is."

He got up to leave. "Thanks for the interesting fruit. Maybe I could take a few seeds back with me when I go."

"Take a whole basketful if you like. By the way—I saw you talking with Lou yesterday. Do you have any suggestions on what we might do with him?"

"I think it had better be a cesarean."

Our son Will spent his last vacation weekend at home with us—he would soon be moving into a dormitory at Columbia for the fall semester. A premed student, he was employed for the summer as an orderly at MPI.

When he paid his first visit to the hospital five years ago and met Giselle, Will immediately announced that he wanted to be a reporter. That enthusiasm gradually faded over the years, as youthful interests tend to do, and after several return visits he declared his intention to follow his old man's footsteps right into psychiatry. I am very proud and happy that he made this choice, not just because he would be carrying on a family tradition, but also because he has a natural ability to get along with patients and they with him.

In fact, it was Will who solved a bewildering problem for us earlier in the summer, an elderly man who was pretending to swallow his medication, devising various clever methods and schemes to fool the nurses. Will caught him at it, but, with an understanding beyond his years, did not try to force the man to take his pills or report him for not doing so. Instead, he spoke to him at length about the matter, discovering, finally, that the old boy was afraid to swallow anything red. When we had the medication repackaged in white capsules the patient was home with his family within two weeks.

Will's current self-imposed project, in addition to his regular duties, is to try to decipher the ramblings of a young schizophrenic patient who (Will thinks) is trying to communicate with us through some sort of code that no one can decipher. Most of his utterings seem to be pure gibberish. But occasionally, after one of his meaningless statements, he chomps a few times on an imaginary cigar and repeats the whole thing two or three times. Here is one of Dustin's orations (a kind of poetry?), delivered with four chomps and four repeats, and carefully recorded by Will:

Your life sure is fun when you like cabbage but be careful when you find a yellow box full of crabs or ostrich poop because then the world will stop and you can never really know if this is where someone says that you must comply because you're not going there to learn how to be grateful or to make mistakes when you're stepping out. . . .

Did Dustin have some sort of cabbage fetish, or had he had an unfortunate run-in with a crab or an ostrich? And was the cigar a phallic symbol? We stared at this nonsense for an hour after dinner until Karen sent us outside to shoot a few baskets and chase after the dogs and forget about work for a while. But Will wanted to know more about some of the other schizophrenics and the nature of the affliction in general, which he referred to as "split personality."

"The first thing you should know about schizophrenia is that although it literally means 'split brain,' it is *not* the same thing as multiple personality disorder. It's more of a malfunction of sense and logic, not a 'split' personality. The patient might hear voices, for example, or believe things that are patently false. Others suffer from delusions of grandiosity. In the paranoid type, feelings of persecution predominate. Many speak 'word salad,' but this can happen with certain other maladies, too."

"You're lecturing again, Dad."

"Sorry. I guess I still find it hard to believe you're following in the old man's footsteps."

"It's a dirty job, but somebody's got to do it."

"Anyway, with schizophrenia, you've got to be careful with your diagnosis. Nice shot."

"What's the etiology?"

"Schizophrenia usually develops early in life. Recent evidence suggests a genetic origin, or possibly fetal damage by a virus. It often responds almost miraculously to antipsychotic drugs, but sometimes doesn't, and there's no way to predict which cases—Oxie, come back here with that!"

"What about Dustin?"

"In Dustin's case, none of the neuroleptics has alleviated his symptoms in the slightest, not even a gram of Clozapine a day. But he's an unusual case anyway. I'm sure you've noticed that he plays chess and other games without any problem. He never says much, but he seems perfectly focused and logical during these encounters. In fact, he almost always wins."

"Do you think his problem has anything to do with the games he plays?"

"Who knows?"

"Maybe his parents. They visit him almost every evening. Would it be all right if I talk with them sometime?"

"Now, Will, I admire your enthusiasm, but that's something you shouldn't get involved with at this point."

"Well, I'm not giving up on him. The key to the whole thing is in that cigar routine, I think."

I was very proud of him for his perseverance, which is one of the most important attributes a psychiatrist can have. He spends part of his lunch hours and every spare minute of his time with Dustin. Of course he is quite taken with prot, too, as is everyone, but he gets little chance to talk with him because the line is so long. It's only when everyone else goes off to bed that our alien friend gets any time to himself. I only wished I knew what he was thinking about during those long, dark hours of the night.

SESSION TWENTY

Contrary to popular belief, physicians do not hesitate to criticize each other's work, at least in private. Thus, at the regular Monday-morning staff meeting, considerable doubt was expressed about whether a simple post-hypnotic suggestion (the whistle) would summon Robert from the depths of hell. One of my colleagues, Carl Thorstein, went so far as to call it a "nutty" idea (Carl has often been a thorn in my side, but he's a good psychiatrist). On the other hand, it was generally agreed that little could be lost by doing the experiment, which had not been tried before.

Nor was there much enthusiasm for Giselle's plan to get prot to talk to animals, though the broader suggestion of a zoo outing for the inmates was well received, and I was nominated a committee of one to look into the matter. Villers admonished me "to keep ze costs as low as possible."

Some of the staff members were on vacation, so there

was little further discussion of patients and their progress, if any. However, Virginia Goldfarb mentioned a remarkable improvement in one of her charges, the histrionic narcissistic dancer we call "Rudolph Nureyev."

Rudolph was an only child who was reminded constantly that he was perfect in every way, and getting better. When he decided to take up ballet his parents responded with high praise and strong financial support. With that kind of encouragement (and considerable talent), he went on to become one of America's finest dancers.

His only problem was one of attitude. He expected everyone, even music directors and choreographers, to defer to his impeccable taste and judgment. Eventually he became so important (in his own mind) that he began to voice other demands, and finally became so impossible to work with that he was fired by the management of his dance company. When this news spread, no one else in the world would take him in. He ended up a voluntary patient at MPI when his last and only friend encouraged him to seek professional help.

His sudden improvement came about following a single lengthy conversation with prot, who described to Rudolph the breathtaking beauty and grace of the performers in a balletlike dance he had seen on the planet J-MUT. He encouraged Rudolph to try some of the steps, but it required such fantastic speed, exquisite timing, and contortion of limb that Rudolph found the work impossible to execute. He suddenly realized that he was not the greatest dancer in the universe. Goldfarb reported that his supreme arrogance had vanished immediately, and she was thinking of moving him to Ward One. There was no objection.

Beamish, peering at me over his tiny glasses, joked that we should give prot an office and send all the patients to him. Ron Menninger (no relation to the famous clinic) remarked, a little less facetiously, that perhaps I ought to delay Robert's treatment until prot had done whatever he could for the other inmates, a notion I had grappled with myself.

Villers reminded us that we were expecting three distinguished visitors over the next month or so, including the chair of our board of directors, one of the wealthiest men in America. Klaus wasted no words in emphasizing the importance of this visit, suggesting that we put our very best feet forward that day, funding efforts for the new wing having fallen below expectations.

After some other matters were disposed of, he announced that a major TV network had offered the hospital a healthy sum for an exclusive appearance by prot on one of its talk shows. Astonished by this ridiculous prospect, I asked how they even knew he had returned. Someone pointed out that it had already been picked up by the media, including one of the national news programs. I wondered whether Klaus himself had anything to do with that.

The discussion ended without resolution. Some, like me, thought it preposterous to let one of our patients be interviewed on television. Others, noting that prot was unique in all the world and that he would undoubtedly be able to hold his own with any interviewer, weren't so sure. Though we could certainly use the money, I thought we were opening another can of worms. I pointed out that we had a lot of bizarre and interesting cases at the hospital, so why not a whole TV series based on their individual stories? Villers, missing the irony of my remark, seemed quite enthusiastic. I could almost see dollar signs in his eyes, which lit up like shooting stars as he contemplated the potential windfall.

Virginia caught me after the meeting. She wanted to know whether prot might be willing to schedule a look at a couple of her other patients. She wasn't joking—Goldfarb never jokes. I assured her I would speak to him about the matter.

If I have more than cottage cheese and crackers for lunch I have a hard time staying awake the rest of the afternoon. I watched in envy as Villers put away a huge plate of roast beef, various kinds of vegetables, buttered rolls, and pie. He said very little as he gobbled down his food, and left as soon as he was finished, dots of gravy and piecrust flecking his goatee. As I watched him go, I thought: I don't know much about this man, who keeps his personal life to himself, but I'd know those drooping shoulders anywhere.

Klaus Villers is a paradox of the highest order. He exemplifies, I suppose, the public image of the typical psychiatrist—cold, decisive, analytical. Nothing appears to faze him. I have never seen the slightest hint of shock or amusement on his weather-beaten countenance, rarely sensed even the slightest emotion. Yet, for all his gruffness of character and outspoken opinions he can be soft as an oyster inside.

Perhaps the best example of this is the case of a former patient whom Klaus was powerless to help (a not infrequent situation at MPI). The man, a hopeless manic depressive from a poor family, was so fond of his doctor, for reasons of his own, that he carved several beautiful little birds for Klaus and his wife. When the man died, our "heartless" director, who barely found time or inclination to thank the man for his gifts, paid for his interment out of his own pocket, erecting a huge marker for "The Birdman of MPI." No one knows why he did this, but I choose to believe that he simply felt sorry for a long-suffering patient he could do nothing for.

Klaus emigrated with his family to America from Austria more than fifty years ago. Born in 1930, he grew up during the years preceding World War II. His awareness of the atrocities going on around him may have been a factor in his decision to become a doctor, but this is pure speculation on my part. I don't even know how he met his wife Emma.

For all his intelligence he still maintains a thick German accent and, unbelievably, his wife speaks almost no English at all. Extremely introverted, she virtually never leaves their secluded home on Long Island, tending to her garden and homemaking for herself and her husband. They rarely attend extramural functions or, even after he became director in 1990, invite anyone to their lovely home (I was there only once, years ago). Apparently they see no need for social contacts, finding everything they need in each other. As far as I know they have no children.

Their only hobby is hiking. They have walked the Appalachian Trail many times, once or twice with the late Supreme Court Justice William O. Douglas, who apparently didn't have many friends either. As a result, Klaus knows every species of bird in eastern North America by sight or sound and, in fact, usually spends a part of his lunch hour each day on the lawn watching and listening. He remarked once that his wife does the same thing at exactly the same time so that, in a sense, they enjoy the experience together even though they are miles apart.

The reason I mention this now is that I had not seen him on the lawn with his field glasses for some time, or heard him whistle a bird call as he strode the corridors. In fact, he seemed to be acting a bit strangely in a number of ways, not the least of which was his plan to raise funds for the new wing (his legacy?) by getting prot to go on television. I suspected he was suffering from a mild case of depression, perhaps due to his having reached the standard retirement age of sixty-five. Or maybe he was just over-worked—my own tenure as acting director was the most difficult period of my life.

I wanted to come right out and ask him if there was anything I could do to lighten his load, but I knew that would get nowhere. Besides, I had enough problems without adding him to my already overcrowded schedule.

When I returned to my office I found Giselle sitting in my chair, her feet resting on the stack of papers covering my desk, oblivious to her surroundings. "Giselle, you can't have my desk. You're only here because—"

"I think I know when he's leaving."

"You do? When?"

"About the middle of September."

"How do you know that?"

"When I said there may be a trip to the zoo in the next couple of weeks, he said, 'I can just make it. Count me in.'"

"Okay. Good. Keep it up. Do you have any idea yet who he's taking with him when he leaves?"

"He won't say a word about that. Says he has to work out some details. But it could be anyone."

"That's what I was afraid of. Anything else?"

"I need a place to spread out."

"C'mon. Let's see if we can find you a desk somewhere."

"All right," I said, after watching prot devour a half-dozen oranges. "Let's get to work."

"You call this work? Sitting around chatting and eating fruit? It's a picnic!"

"Yes, I know your thoughts about work. Now—is Robert there with you?"

"Yep, he's right nearby."

"Good. I'd like him to come out for a while."

"What—without your hypnosis trick?"

"Robert? May I speak with you please?"

Prot sighed, set aside the ragged remains of an orange, and gazed dully at the ceiling.

"Robert? This is very important. Please come out for a moment. Everything will be all right. No harm will come to you or to anyone. . . ."

But prot just sat there with his know-it-all smirk. "You're wasting your time, gino. One, two—hey—where's the dot?"

"I'm not going to hypnotize you just yet."

"Why not?"

"I've got another idea."

"Will wonders never cease!"

I reached into my shirt pocket and pulled out the whistle. Prot watched me with amusement as I put it to my lips and blew. At that moment the smirk vanished and a different person appeared, only I wasn't sure who it was. He wasn't slouched in the chair as Robert usually is. "Robert?"

"I'm here, Dr. Brewer. I've been waiting for you to call." Though he seemed quite unhappy about it, he was nonetheless there, apparently ready to talk.

I stared at him, savoring the moment. It was the first time I had ever seen Robert when he wasn't catatonic or under hypnosis (with rare exceptions—see *K-PAX*). But the triumph was undercut by a hint of suspicion. Something wasn't right—it seemed too easy. On the other hand, he had been pondering his dilemma for years, and perhaps, as sometimes happens, he was simply getting bored with living in a figurative straitjacket. "How are you feeling?"

"Not so hot." He looked much like prot, of course, but there were dissimilarities. For example, he was far more serious, not the least bit cocky. His voice was a little different. And he seemed exhausted.

"I can understand that. I hope we can help you feel better soon."

"That would be nice."

"Let me ask you first: Should I call you Robert or Rob?"

"My family calls me Robin. My friends call me Rob."

"May I call you Rob?"

"If you like."

"Thank you. Care for some fruit?"

"No, thanks. I'm not hungry."

There were so many questions I wanted to ask him that I didn't know where to begin. "Do you know where you are?"

"Yes."

"How do you know that?"

"Prot told me."

"Where is prot right now?"

"He's waiting."

"Can you speak with him?"

"Yes."

"Good. Now—do you know where you've been for the past five years?"

"In my room."

"But you couldn't move and you couldn't speak to us—do you remember?"

"Yes."

"Were you able to hear us?"

"Yes. I heard everything."

"Can you tell me why you couldn't speak or respond in some way?"

"I *wanted* to. But I just couldn't."

"Do you know why?"

"I was afraid to."

"Why were you afraid?"

"I was afraid . . ." He gazed off into some inner space. "I was afraid of what might happen."

"All right. We'll get back to that later. Let me just ask you this: You seem to be less fearful now than you were then—can you tell me why?"

He started to answer, then hesitated.

"Take your time."

"There are a couple of reasons."

"I would like very much to hear them, Rob, if you feel like telling me."

"Well, all of you have been so kind to me since I came here that I guess I felt like I owed you something."

62

"Thank you. I'm glad you feel that way. And the other reason?"

"He said I can trust you."

"Prot? Why now, and not before?"

"Because he's leaving soon, and I think he's becoming impatient with me."

"How soon? Do you know?"

"No."

"All right. But you were in the same situation five years ago. How is it different this time?"

"Last time I knew he would be coming back. This time he's not."

"He's not coming back? How do you know that?"

"He doesn't like it here."

"I know, but—"

"He told me you would take his place. That you would help me when he's gone."

He was appealing to me with such intensity that I went over and placed my hand on his shoulder. "I will, Rob. Believe me, I'll help you in every way I can."

With that he slowly puckered his face and began to cry. "I'm so tired of feeling bad. You don't know how bad it is." His head dropped.

"No one who's not in your shoes can understand what you've been through, Rob. But we've helped a lot of people in similar situations and I think you're going to feel better very soon."

His head lifted and he looked at me. He was no longer crying. "Thanks, dr. b. I feel better already."

"Prot? Where's Robert?"

"He's kind of tired. But if you play a nice tune on your whistle he might be back later."

"Uh—prot?"

"Hmmmmmmmm?"

"Thank you."

"For what?"

"For giving him the confidence to come out."

"Did he tell you that?"

"Yes. And he also told me this might be your last visit to Earth. Is that true?"

"It is if you get Robert back on his feet. Then there wouldn't be any need for me to come, would there?"

"No, there wouldn't. In fact, it might be better if you didn't."

"Don't worry—I know when I'm not wanted. Besides, there are a lot of other interesting places to go."

"Other planets?"

"Yep. Billions and billions of them in this GALAXY alone. You'd be surprised."

"Can you give us a little time before you go back? Can you give us six more weeks?"

"I can only give you what I've got."

"Will you at least tell me how much you've got?"

"Nope."

"But prot—Robert's life is at stake. Which is why you're here, isn't it?"

"I told you before: I'll give you some warning. It won't come as a complete surprise."

"I'm happy to hear that," I said glumly. "All right. Well, as long as you're here, I'd like to ask you one more thing about Rob."

"Is that a promise?"

"Not exactly. Now—is there some other reason he's suddenly speaking to me? Anything I don't know?"

"There doesn't seem to be any limit to what you don't know, my human friend. But I will tell you this: Don't be fooled by his cheery disposition. It was all he could do to come forward today. He still has a long way to go and he could retreat at a moment's notice. Be gentle with him."

"I'll do my very best, prot."

"In spite of your primitive methods? Lotsa luck." He picked up the fragment of orange and stuffed it into his mouth.

"How are you doing with the letters, by the way?"

Through orange teeth: "I've read most of them."

"Any decisions yet?"

"Too soon for that."

"Will you tell me when you've decided who's going back with you?"

"I might. Or maybe I'll save it for the tv show."

"What? Who told you about that?"

"Everyone knows about that."

"I see. And I suppose everyone knows about the trip to the zoo? And about all the people who want to talk to you?"

"Of course."

"Prot?"

"Yeah, coach?"

"You're driving me crazy."

"Tell me about it," he sighed.

Thinking he was joking, I chuckled a little. But he seemed to be quite serious. I glanced at the clock on the wall behind him—we still had a few minutes left. I stood up. "All right. You take my place and I'll take yours."

Without a moment's hesitation he jumped up and ran over to my chair. He plopped into it, squeezed the vinyl arms several times, and whirled around in a complete circle. Obviously enjoying himself, he grabbed a yellow pad and began to scribble furiously as he stroked an imaginary beard.

I took his chair. "You're supposed to ask me some questions," I prodded.

"That won't be necessary," he mumbled.

"Why not?"

"Because I already know what's bugging you."

"I'd love to hear what it is."

"Alimentary, my dear canal. You were born on a mean, cruel PLANET from which you see no way to escape. You're trapped here at the mercy of your fellow humans. That would drive any being crazy." Suddenly he banged his fist on the arm of my chair. "Time's up!" He scooted over, grabbed another orange, and bit into it. Then he whirled again and flung his feet onto my desk. "And I've got work to do," he concluded with a dismissive wave. "Pay the cashier on your way out."

I gave him a poor imitation of a Cheshire-cat grin. He screeched and bolted for the door.

It wasn't until later that I happened to glance at the yellow pad he had scribbled on. In a messy but legible scrawl he had written, over and over again, 17:18/9/20. It took me a moment to figure it out, but finally I realized: He's leaving on the twentieth at 5:18 P.M.!

Not having been in Ward Three since before my "vacation," I decided to take a brief tour. I found Michael in 3A perusing a book called *The Right to Die*, a work he has read dozens of times, as Russell reads and rereads the New Testament.

A naked woman streaked by. Michael ignored her. He wanted to know when he was going to get to talk with prot. Unforgivably, his request had slipped my mind, but I told him I would see to it immediately. He said, jokingly, I hoped, "I could be dead by the time he gets here." I slapped him on the shoulder and continued my rounds, stopping to chat with various social and sexual deviates, tortured souls preoccupied with specific bodily functions. I watched in never-ending amazement as one of them, a Japanese-American male, undressed himself, smelled the crotch of his underwear, then dressed again, and undressed, over and over again. Another man kept trying to kiss my hand. Others performed their own endless rituals and compulsions. Yet none of these miserable creatures were more tragic than the inhabitants of 3B, the severely autistic ward.

Autism was once blamed principally on unfeeling and uncaring parents, especially the mother. It is now known that autists suffer some sort of brain defect, whether genetic or induced by organic disease, and no amount of nurturing will alter the progress of this debilitating affliction.

Stated simply, autists are missing the part of brain function that makes a person a soulful human being, someone who can relate to other people. Although often able to perform extraordinary feats, they appear to do so entirely mechanically without any "feel" for what they have accomplished. The ability of the autist to concentrate on whatever it is that occupies his or her thoughts is astonishing, and typically to the exclusion of everything else. There are exceptions, of course, and some are able to hold jobs and learn to function to some extent in society. Most, however, live in worlds of their own.

I found our twenty-one-year-old engineering wizard, whom I'll call Jerry, working on a matchstick re-creation of the Golden Gate Bridge. It was almost finished. On display nearby were replicas of the Capitol Building, the Eiffel Tower, the Taj Mahal. I watched him for a while. He worked deftly and rapidly, yet seemed to pay little attention to his project. His eyes darted all over the room, his mind apparently somewhere else. He used no notes or models, but worked from memory of photographs he had glanced at only briefly.

To Jerry, who may not even have noticed me, I said, "That's beautiful. How long before it's finished?"

"Before it's finished," he replied, without changing his pace.

"What's next on the agenda?"

"Agenda. Agenda. Agenda. Agenda. Agenda. Agenda—"

"Well, I've got to go now."

"Go now. Go now. Go now."

"Bye, Jer."

"Bye, Jer."

And so it was with the others, most of whom were wandering around or staring intently at their fingertips or studying the blemishes on the walls. Sometimes someone would let out a bark or start clapping his hands, but not one of them paid the slightest attention to me or glanced in my direction. It is as if autists actively practice a kind of desperate avoidance. Nevertheless, we continue to try to find some way to relate to them, to enter their worlds, to bring them into ours.

One feels sorry for such individuals, to pity their lack of contact with other human beings. Yet, for all we know, they may be quite happy within the confines of their private realms, which might, in fact, encompass gigantic universes filled with an incredible variety of shapes and relationships, with interesting and satisfying visions, and tastes and sounds and smells that the rest of us cannot even imagine. It would be fascinating to enter such a world for one glorious moment. Whether we would choose to stay there, however, is another matter.

SESSION TWENTY-ONE

S till trying to come to grips with what I suspected was prot's upcoming "departure" date, I took a stroll on the grounds, where a spirited game of croquet was in progress, though what rules were in force was impossible to determine. Behind this circus I spotted Klaus over by the sunflowers talking animatedly with Cassandra, a woman in her mid-forties who has the ability to forecast certain events with uncanny accuracy. How she does this is anybody's guess, including her own. The problem with Cassandra is that she has no interest in anything else. By the time she was brought to us she had nearly starved to death. Her first words, after she had seen the lawn with its plethora of chairs and benches from which she could contemplate the heavens, were, "I think I'm going to like it here."

One of the areas in which she excels is that of weather. Perhaps this is because she's outdoors so much, winter and summer. If you've ever heard the five-day forecasts of the shameless TV weather people, you know that their predictions are very often wrong. Cassie, on the other hand, is usually right for periods of up to two weeks from the date of her prognostication. I had heard, in fact, that Villers, her staff physician, had consulted her about conditions for the proposed outing to the zoo before he would allow a date to be set. (When Milton heard that fair weather was expected for the trip, he remarked, "Only fair? Surely we should wait until it gets better.")

Animals also seem to know when changes in the weather are coming, possibly because of some unknown sensitivity to subtle variations in air pressure or humidity, though not so far in advance, probably. But how can we explain her uncanny ability to predict, with more than ninety-percent accuracy, who will become the next president or the winner of the Super Bowl, weeks or even months beforehand, something no animal can do. (It is rumored that Villers has reaped a small fortune from her desultory pronouncements, which he usually keeps to himself, claiming doctor-patient privilege.) What does she see in the sun and stars that the rest of us are missing?

I also saw Frankie waddling around the lawn under her usual black cloud. Her inability to form human relationships seems to be related in some way to autism—perhaps a similar part of the brain is involved. Unlike the true autists, however, she has no problem communicating with the staff and her fellow patients, though what she conveys is likely to be a caustic comment or jarring insult. Whether these jabs are intentional I can't say, but she was one patient I hoped prot might be able to help, despite his own misgivings about human love.

At the far corner I noticed several of the other inmates grouped under the big oak tree, shading themselves like a bunch of sheep from the heat of the August sun, except that they were all facing inward. I wondered whether something had happened. But when I started in their direction I saw prot in their midst. He was holding forth on some subject or other, commanding their complete attention. Even Russell was silent. As I approached them my beeper squealed.

I hurried to a phone and punched the number of the departmental office. "It's Robert Porter's mother," the operator said. "Can you take the call?" I asked him to transfer it.

Mrs. Porter had received my letter and understandably wanted to know how Robert was doing. Unfortunately, I could only tell her that I was pleased with his progress so far, but that much more work remained to be done. She asked when she could come to see him. I told her I would let her know the moment her son was well enough for that. She seemed disappointed, of course, but agreed to wait for further progress. (I didn't mention the possibility that she might instead find him in the same state he was in when she was here five years ago.)

I returned to the lawn. Villers had departed, leaving Cassandra to gaze once more at the heavens. Prot was gone, too, and the others were milling around under the oak tree, directionless without their magnetic leader. Frankie was still off by herself, cursing the wind.

"Dr. Flynn was here yesterday with another astronomer and a physicist," Giselle told me over lunch in the staff dining room. "I gave him an hour with prot. I've never seen anybody so eager to meet someone. He actually ran down the corridor to prot's room."

"Well, did he learn anything he didn't know before?"

"He didn't get everything he wanted, but he seemed to think it was worth the trip."

"Why didn't he get everything he wanted?"

"Prot's afraid he'll use the information to his own selfish ends."

"I figured as much. Of course it's also possible that prot doesn't know all the answers."

"I wouldn't count on it."

"What sorts of things did Flynn ask him about?"

She took an enormous bite of a sandwich and continued, her jaw the size of an apple, "For one thing, he wanted to know how old the universe is."

"How old is it?"

"Infinitely."

"What?"

"You remember—it keeps expanding and contracting, forever and ever."

"Oh. Right."

"Flynn wasn't satisfied with that. He asked him how long the present expansion has been going on."

"What did prot tell him?"

"He said, 'How do you know it's expanding?' Flynn started to explain the Doppler effect but prot cut him short with: 'When the UNIVERSE is in the contraction phase you'll still have the same Doppler shift.' Flynn said, 'That's ridiculous.' Prot said, 'Spoken like a true homo sapiens.' "

"Anything else?"

"Yes. He wanted to know how many planets there are in our galaxy, and how many of them are inhabited."

"What did prot say?"

She swallowed some of the food bulging in her cheek. "He said there are a trillion planets in our galaxy alone, and a proportionate number in all the others. And guess what percentage of these are inhabited."

"Half of them?"

"Not *that* many. Point two percent."

"Is that all?"

"All? That means there are several billion planets and moons in the Milky Way teeming with life."

"How many of these creatures are like us?"

"That's the interesting thing. According to prot, a lot of the beings around the universe resemble us. 'Us' being mammals, birds, fish, and so on."

"What about humans?"

"He says that humanoid beings have arisen or are evolving on some of these, but that they usually don't last very long. About a hundred thousand of our years, on the average."

"Not a very pleasant prospect."

"Not for us."

"What else?"

"Dr. Flynn wanted to know how we can accomplish hydrogen fusion as an energy source."

"And prot wouldn't tell him, right?"

"Oh, he told him, all right."

"Really? What's the secret?"

"You won't believe it."

"Probably not."

"It only works with a certain substance as catalyst."

"What substance?"

"Something found on Earth only in spider excrement."

"You're kidding."

"But it's not just any old spider poop."

"It's not?"

"Nope. Only that from a particular species indigenous to Libya. The stuff comes in little gold pellets the size of poppy seeds!" She started to giggle.

"Is this prot's idea of a joke?"

"Flynn didn't think so. He's already trying to figure out how to get into Libya." Then she became more serious. "Guess what else?"

"I can't imagine."

"He wanted prot to give him a demonstration of light-travel."

I finished the last tiny curd of cottage cheese. "Did he comply?"

"Yes."

"What? He disappeared again?"

"Not exactly. He got out his little flashlight and his mirror, but just then a cat ran by. It meowed, and everybody turned to look at it for a second. When we looked back, he was on the other side of the room. Dr. Flynn was flabbergasted. So was I. I had never seen him do that before." Her eyes were bright as a squirrel's.

I couldn't hide my skepticism. "Sounds like a pretty neat trick."

"Dr. B, do you know anyone else who can do that trick?"

"Well, did prot tell him how it's done?"

"No. He said we're not 'ready' for light-travel."

"I figured as much."

Another bite and the cheek swelled up again. "Then the physicist jumped in. That got pretty hairy. She asked prot about all kinds of alpha and omega stuff. I'll have to do some studying to figure it all out. But one thing I understood."

"What's that?"

"You ever hear of quarks?"

"They're supposed to be the fundamental particles of atomic nuclei, aren't they?"

"Mm-hm. But inside of them are smaller particles and inside of them still smaller ones."

"Good God. Where does it all end?"

"It doesn't."

"What did the physicist think of all this?"

"She wanted the details."

"Did prot give her any?"

"Nope. He said that would spoil the fun of discovering them for herself."

"Maybe he doesn't know any of the details. Maybe he's just speculating."

"He knows enough to travel at superlight speed!"

"Maybe. Anything else?"

"That's about it. They left a thick notebook of additional questions for prot to consider."

I told her about my suspicion that he only had until September 20 to answer them. She nodded unhappily. "And what about the letters? Has prot said anything about the letters?"

"He's finished with them. He gave them back to me."

"He doesn't want them?"

"Whatever he wanted from them is in his head some-where. Of course more keep coming in. He gets some every day."

"And where are the old ones?"

"They're on the little table you gave me to use as a desk." She drew out and emphasized the word "little." "You want to read them?"

"Isn't it illegal for me to read them?"

"Not if he gives you permission."

"Would he do that, do you think?"

"He already has. I'll put them on the *big* desk in your office."

"Not all of them. Just leave me a representative sample. By the way—the faculty thinks the idea of a trip to the zoo is a pretty good one. Can you contact the officials over there and set it up?"

"I know someone who works there. All I need from you is a definite date."

"Gino! Long time no see!"

"It's only been two days, prot."

"That's a long time. You can get halfway across some GALAXIES in two of your days."

"Maybe *you* could."

"So could you if you wanted to badly enough. But you're

more concerned with other things. The stock market, for example."

"But you won't tell us how to do it."

"I just did."

"Uh-huh. Anything else you feel like telling me before we begin?"

"I think some of my correspondents would enjoy a long voyage."

"Who wants to go, for example?" I casually asked him.

"Your humor still needs work, gene."

"I mean in general."

"Those who are unhappy here on EARTH."

"That's not much help."

He shrugged.

"All right. Are you finished with your grape juice?"

"Yep. Amazing stuff. Nothing in the UNIVERSE purpler than grape juice."

"Okay. Remember the whistle?"

"Of course. But that won't be necessary, Dr. Brewer."

The transition had been so subtle that I barely noticed the slight change in voice and manner, especially with the purple mustache across his upper lip. "Robert?"

"Yes."

"How are you feeling?"

"I don't know. Strange. Shaky. Not too bad, I guess."

"I'm glad to hear that. Tell me—can you come out whenever you want to now?"

"I always could. I just—couldn't."

"I understand. Will you be able to stay here for a while?"

"If you like."

"Good. As I told you under hypnosis, this is your safe

haven. Please try to remember that. Now—is there anything you especially want to talk about today? Anything bothering you right this minute?"

"I miss my wife and my little girl."

I was astonished by this simple sentence. Coming from anyone else it would have been routine and long overdue. But I thought it might take weeks to get him to talk about his family. This was a profound change. How much courage it must have taken for Robert to say it! "I'd like to hear more about them if you're ready to tell me."

His eyes drifted away and became moist and dreamy. It was as if he wanted to dwell lovingly on a delightful subject for a moment before beginning. At last he said, "We had a wonderful place in the country, with a garden and a small orchard. None of the trees had produced any fruit yet, but they would have in another year or two. We had five whole acres with a hedgerow and a small pond and a stream and lots of maples and birches. Prot told me it reminded him of K-PAX, except there's hardly any water there. The whole thing was full of life. Birds and rabbits and groundhogs and some goldfish in the pond. We had daffodils and tulips and forsythia. It was beautiful in the spring and fall. And the winter, too, when the snow came. Sally loved winter. We used to do some cross-country skiing and Becky liked to skate around on the little pond. She loved all the birds and the other animals, too. She fed the deer. The house wasn't very big, but it was just about right for us. Sally couldn't have any more children. . . ." He paused for a few moments, remembering.

"We had a big fireplace and Becky had her own room with flowered wallpaper and enough space for all her things. She had some pictures taped to the walls. Rock stars, I guess. I never got much into rock and roll. The kitchen—" He broke off suddenly and his jaw seemed to clamp shut. "The kitchen—"

"That's all right, Rob. We can come back to the kitchen later."

"Why should we do that? Are you still hungry?"

"Prot! Where's Robert?"

"He's right here, collecting himself. Didn't I tell you to be more gentle with him?"

"Listen, my alien friend. I know what I'm doing. Robert has made remarkable progress since you've been back. Give him a chance."

He shrugged. "Just don't push too hard, doc. He's dancing as fast as he can."

"Are you going to let him come back, or not?"

"Just give him a minute or two. He's been trying to forget everything for a long time. It's hard for him to cough it up on demand."

"I haven't demanded anything."

"Could we talk about something else for a while?"

It took me a moment to realize that Robert had returned. "Whatever you want to talk about is fine with me, Rob."

"I don't know what to say."

"Let's go back a little. Would you like to tell me more about your boyhood? Last time we stopped when you were twelve, I believe."

"Twelve. I was in the seventh grade."

"Did you like school?"

"I hate to admit it, but I loved it."

"Why do you hate to admit it?"

"Everybody's supposed to hate school. But I liked it. I remember the seventh grade because that was the first year we went to different rooms for different classes."

"What classes did you like best?"

"General science. Biology. We had a field and woods behind our house, and I used to walk around there and try to identify all the different trees and things. That was great."

"Did you do that with a friend? Or one of your sisters?"

"No, I usually went by myself."

"Did you like to be by yourself?"

"I didn't mind. But I had friends, too. We played basketball and messed around together. Smoked cigarettes up in the tree house. But none of them cared about my field or the woods. So I usually went there by myself. I can still remember the way the trees smelled on a hot summer day, or the ground after a rain. The crickets at night. I saw deer sometimes early in the mornings and around sunset. I watched them and found out where they slept. They didn't know I was watching them. I used to go there in the evenings sometimes and wait for them to wake up, and then I'd see where they would go."

"What about Sally? Did you know her then?"

"Yes. Ever since first grade."

"What did you think of her?"

"I thought she was the prettiest girl in school. She had hair like the sun."

"Did you talk to her much?"

"No. I wanted to, but I was too shy. Anyway, she didn't pay much attention to me. She was a cheerleader and everything."

"When did she first begin to pay some attention to you?"

"When we were juniors. I was on the wrestling team. She started coming to the matches. I couldn't figure out why she did that, but I tried very hard to impress her."

"Did you succeed?"

"I guess so. One day she told me she thought I had some good moves. That was when I asked her to go to the movies with me. It was our first date."

"What did you see?"

"*The Sting.*"

"That's a terrific film."

Rob nodded. "I'll never forget it."

"When was your next date?"

"Not for quite a while."

"Why not?"

"Like I said, I was shy. Sally had other friends. I wasn't sure she liked me that much. I couldn't understand why she would."

"How did you find out she did?"

"If you've ever lived in a small town you know how word gets around. She told someone, and *she* told someone, and so on until it got back to me that she liked me a lot and wanted to go out with me again."

"So you finally asked her for another date?"

"Not exactly. She finally gave up and asked me."

"What did you think about that?"

"I liked it. I liked *her*. She was so friendly and outgoing. When she was with you she made you feel like you were the only other person in the world."

"And eventually you fell in love with her."

"I think I was always in love with her. I used to dream about her all the time."

"You got the girl of your dreams!"

Thoughtfully: "Yes, I guess I did." He produced a sickly smile. "I'm lucky, aren't I?"

"Do you remember any of the dreams?"

"I—I don't think so. . . ."

"All right. We'll talk about that some other time. When did you ask Sally to marry you?"

"On graduation day."

"From high school."

"Yes."

"Weren't there some problems associated with that? Didn't you want to go to college?"

"She was pregnant."

"She was carrying your child?"

"No."

"She wasn't?"

"No."

I was puzzled by this for a moment before I realized what he was saying. I asked, as gently and casually as I could, "Do you happen to know whose child it was?"

"No."

"All right. We'll come back to that later."

"If you say so, coach."

"Prot! You've got to stop popping up like this!"

"It's more like Rob popped down."

"Why didn't you tell me Rebecca wasn't Robert's child?"

"She wasn't?"

"No."

"I didn't know. Anyway, what's the diff?"

"On Earth people like to know who their fathers are."

"Why?"

"Blood is thicker than water."

"So is mucus."

"Just answer me this: Do you have any idea at all who Rebecca's father might be? Did Robert ever mention another boyfriend of Sarah's? Anything like that?"

"No. He didn't call me just to gossip. Anyway, why don't you ask him? He's right here."

"Thanks for the suggestion, but I think we'll call it quits for today. I don't want to push him too hard at this point."

"My dear sir, there may be hope for you yet."

I glanced at the clock. It was exactly three-fifty and there was a seminar at four. The speaker was Dr. Beamish, whose topic, one of his favorites, was "Freud and Homosexuality."

"Before you go, just tell me one more thing: Is Robert all right now?"

"He's okay. He'll probably be ready to talk to you again by Friday."

"Good. Thanks again for all your help."

"No problemo."

He was still wearing the purple mustache as he turned and strode briskly out of my examining room. I had been so caught up in these unexpected developments that I forgot again to ask him whether he would be willing to speak with Mike and some of the other patients.

I didn't go to the seminar. There were several uncomfortable questions sticking like cockleburs to the edges of my mind.

For one thing, Robert had been literally hiding behind prot, barely saying a word for a decade, half of that in a state of catatonia. Now, abruptly, he was out and talking with only minimal encouragement. He *wanted* to talk! Though he retreated when the subject became too painful, he actually seemed fairly comfortable at times, and I wondered whether he had begun to come out in the wards as well (I made a note to check with Betty McAllister on this). It had been a dramatic, remarkable change, one that rarely happens in psychiatry.

For another, Rob attributed his sudden courage to prot's upcoming departure. But multiple personality disorder doesn't operate that way. It is Robert who calls prot into "existence" when he is needed. It would be a peculiar aberration indeed if prot refused to show up, although such a *rara avis* is not unknown in the literature. For example, there is the occasional case of a primary and secondary personality who can't stand each other, and sometimes the latter refuses to show up out of spite or the former declines to ask him to.

But prot and Robert seemed to get along quite well. Still, it occurred to me that the net effect of his leaving would be the same as that resulting from such a "family" spat. Perhaps I could get Robert angry enough with prot that he would be glad to see him depart. But would this help him to face the world on his own, or simply make matters worse?

There were other unanswered questions as well, chief of which was: Who was the father of Sally's child? And what effect did this twist of fate have on Robert's already damaged (by his father's untimely injury and eventual death twelve years earlier) psyche? It was beginning to look like the inside of an atom. Whenever we seemed to be getting somewhere more particles appeared. How deeply would we have to dig before we got to the heart of Robert's problem? And could we get there before the twentieth of September?

I discussed these concerns over dinner with my wife. Her comment was: "Maybe Robert isn't the father, and maybe he is."

I said, "What do you mean?"

"Maybe he can't admit it, even to himself. If you ask me, the key event happened much earlier than that."

"What makes you think so?"

"Well, prot made his first appearance when Robert was six, didn't he? Sometime before that. Maybe you should concentrate on his early childhood."

"I'm dancing as fast as I can, 'Doctor' Brewer!"

When I arrived on Thursday morning I found a stack of "prot" letters on my desk. Some were written by people who might as well have been residents of MPI or another hospital. ("Help! Someone's trying to poison our water with fluoride!") Others had plans to "develop" K-PAX; for example, to turn it into a gigantic theme park called "Utopia." Still others wanted to spread their various religions to the far corners of the universe. But most were pathetically similar. The following is an example of one such letter:

Glen Burnie, Maryland

Dear Mr. Prot:

My son Troy is ten years old. After he saw on TV a story about how you don't kill any animals or eat meat, he won't eat it either. I don't know what to give him. He seems healthy, but I'm afraid he's not getting enough of the vitamines [sic] that you get in meat. He has thrown out all his toy soldiers, too. Now he says he wants to go to K-PAX with you. In fact, he's all packed.

I don't know what to do. Please write to him and explain that you didn't mean that earth people are supposed to be like you.

Thank you.

Yours truly,
Mrs. Floyd B—

Many of the letters were from children themselves, scrawled in large print. The two I saw were typical, I suppose. One pleaded with prot to "please stop all the wars." The other, from an older girl, apologized that she couldn't go to K-PAX now because she had to help out at home, but could she come later? If these were a representative sampling of those that prot had received, there must have been thousands and thousands of children all over the world who were ready and willing to take their chances on an alien planet rather than accept what they had inherited from their forebears. I felt both sadness and elation at the prospects for the future of our own world if these heartfelt letters were any indication of the thoughts and hopes of today's youth.

At the bottom of the stack was a piney note neatly handwritten in green ink: *I want to go, too!*

A peculiar sight: prot and Giselle hurrying through the lounge on their way to the front door, Russell following close behind and, trailing along after him, a bunch of the other patients. And, behind *them*, a string of cats. Milton danced along at the front of the pack, wearing his funny hat and playing an imaginary tin whistle. No one was saying a word. It was almost like a strange, silent dream, an image from a Bergman or Kurosawa film. I noticed that prot was carrying something in his upturned palm.

Not wanting to disturb them, I ran to the front windows and watched as he dropped his cargo onto the lawn, to shouts and applause from his coterie. I couldn't see what it was. It was only later that I learned that prot had found a spider frantically trying to claw its way up the side of one of the bathroom sinks. He and the others had taken it outside. When it disappeared in the grass Russell said a prayer and the whole thing was over.

Russ had been praying a lot lately, even more so than when he believed himself to be Jesus Christ. I'd been told he had decided that the end of the world wasn't far off. Whether this had anything to do with prot's return I couldn't say. In any case, his newfound preoccupation with death and the next world was little different from that of millions of other people walking around loose.

As I watched the group come back through the big door at the end of the lounge, prot and Giselle hand in hand, something occurred to me that I hadn't thought of before, or perhaps chose to ignore. The rebudding romance between them (despite prot's abhorrence of sex) seemed to be getting stronger by the day. How would she take it if prot disappeared and Robert took his place in the world? More to the point, might she try to obstruct Robert's treatment in some way? And would prot's evident fondness for her likewise cause him second thoughts about helping Robert to get well?

SESSION TWENTY-TWO

On the first day of September we were honored by a visit from the chairman of our board of directors. Villers had thoroughly impressed upon everyone the importance of his arrival—the hospital was looking for a donor for whom we would name the badly needed (and still unfunded) new wing. I was awarded the privilege of hosting this distinguished businessman, whose stock portfolio gave him control of several major corporations, a bank, a television network (the one producing prot's talk-show interview, I realized), and other enterprises. Menninger joked that he was so rich he was considering making a run for the presidency. Klaus was determined to get a share of this treasure trove.

My first impression when I met him at the gate was that he must have had a very difficult childhood. Despite his great wealth and commensurate power he was noneffusive almost to the point of disappearing. He reluctantly offered me a hand that was so cold and limp that I instinctively dropped it, as if it were a dead fish. That probably cost us a few thousand, I thought with some dismay. But perhaps he was used to it.

During the entire visit he never looked my way. As we toured the grounds prior to having coffee with Villers and the rest of the executive committee, I noticed that he kept a respectable distance from me, as if to avoid contamination. Indeed, one of his bodyguards stationed himself between us at all times. Furthermore, he seemed to suffer from a mild form of obsessive-compulsive disorder. Whenever we approached anything with a corner on it he would stop and feel the sharp vortex with his thumb before moving on (I had heard that there were no corners anywhere in his office).

Oddly, he seemed discomfited by the sight of the patients milling around, particularly Jackie sitting on the grass, a mound of dirt piling up between her bare legs. Bert, checking for lost valuables behind every tree, and Frankie, who was shuffling around topless to beat the heat, did nothing to ease his consternation. Apparently he had never seen mentally disturbed people before. Or perhaps it was a case of what might easily have been himself.

Nevertheless, everything was going more or less smoothly and according to plan until Manuel loped toward us, squawking and flapping his arms. When I turned to explain to our visitor the problem with this particular patient, I saw him sprinting for the gate. The bodyguards were barely able to keep up with him. I certainly wasn't.

Villers couldn't bring himself to speak to me the entire morning. I didn't get any of the free coffee or little cakes, either. To tell the truth, I holed up in my office for the rest of the forenoon, reorganizing my files and ignoring the phone. But when I saw him at lunch he was positively apoplectic with joy. Our board chairman had sent over a check for one million dollars. More than enough to get our fund-raising program off the ground, and giving him a leg up on a name above the door of the new facility.

Klaus was so delighted, in fact, that he paid for my meal (cottage cheese and crackers), a first for him.

Prot ignored the bowl of fruit when he came into my examining room and I knew that Robert had already come forward without even being asked. "Rob?"

"Hello, Dr. Brewer."

"Is prot with you?"

"He says to go ahead without him."

"That's all right. Maybe we won't need him this time." He shrugged.

"How are you feeling today?"

"Okay."

"Good. I'm happy to hear that. Shall we take up where we left off last time?"

"I guess so." He seemed nervous.

I waited for him to begin. When he didn't, I prodded: "Last time we were talking about your wife and daughter—remember?"

"Yes."

"Is there anything more you'd like to tell me about them?"

"Could we talk about something else?"

"What do you want to talk about?"

"I don't know."

"Would you like to tell me about your father?"

There was a long pause before he replied, "He was a wonderful man. He was more like a friend than a father." Oddly, he seemed to be reciting this, as if he had prepared and rehearsed it.

"You spent a lot of time with him?"

"The year he died we were together all the time."

"Tell me about that."

Almost woodenly: "He was sick. A steer had fallen on him in the slaughterhouse and crushed him. I don't know what all was wrong with him, but it was a lot of things. He was in pain all the time. All the time. He didn't sleep much."

"What sorts of things did you do together?"

"Games, mostly. Hearts, Crazy Eights, Monopoly. He taught me to play chess. He didn't know how to play, but he learned and then he taught me."

"Could you beat him?"

"He let me beat him a few times."

"How old were you then?"

"Six."

"Did you play any chess later on?"

"A little in high school."

"Were you any good?"

"Not too bad."

This gave me an idea (I had checked with Betty, and also Giselle: Robert had not yet made an appearance in the wards). "Some of the other patients play chess. Would you like a game sometime?"

He hesitated. "I don't know. Maybe. . . ."

"We'll wait until you're ready. Okay—what else can you tell me about your father?"

Again as if by rote: "Mom got him a book on astronomy from the library. We learned a lot of the constellations. He had a pair of binoculars and we looked at the moon and planets. We even saw four of Jupiter's moons with them."

"That must've been something."

"It was. It made the planets and stars seem not so far away. Like it would be easy to get there."

"Tell me something about that. What did you think it would be like on another planet?"

"I thought it would be fantastic. Daddy told me that all kinds of different creatures might live there, but that most of them would be nicer than people were. That there wouldn't be any crime, or any wars, and everyone would get along fine. There wouldn't be any sickness either, or poverty or injustice. I felt sorry that we were stuck here, and that he was always hurting so much and nobody could do anything about it. But when we were outside at night looking up at the stars he seemed to feel better. Those were the best times. . . ." Rob gazed dreamily at the ceiling.

"What else did you do?"

Shakily (he was almost in tears) he replied, "We watched TV sometimes. And we talked. He got me a dog. A big, shaggy dog. He was red. I called him 'Apple.'"

"What sorts of things did you talk about?"

"Nothing special. You know—what it was like when he was growing up, stuff like that. He taught me to do things, like how to pound a nail and saw a board. He showed me how the car's engine worked. He was my friend and my protector. But then—" I waited for him to come to grips with his thoughts. At last he said, as though he still couldn't believe it, "But then he died."

"Were you there when that happened?"

Robert's head jerked to the side. "No."

"Where were you?"

He turned back toward me, but his eyes avoided my gaze. "I—I don't remember. . . ."

"What's the next thing you remember?"

"The day of the funeral. Prot was there." He was starting to fidget in his chair.

"All right. Let's talk about something else for a moment." He sighed deeply and the squirming stopped.

"What was it like when you were younger, before your father was injured? Did you spend a lot of time with him then?"

"I don't know. Not as much, I guess."

"Well, how old were you when the accident happened?"

"Five."

"Can you remember anything that happened when you were younger?"

"It's all kind of fuzzy."

"What's the earliest thing you remember?"

"Burning my hand on the stove."

"How old were you then?"

"Three."

"What's the next thing you remember?"

"I remember being chased by a cow."

"How old were you then?"

"It was my fourth birthday. We had a picnic in a field."

"What else happened when you were four?"

"I fell out of the willow tree and broke my arm."

Robert went on to relate a variety of other things that had happened to him when he was four. For example, they moved to a different house. He could recall that day in some detail. By the time he turned five, however, everything became a blank. When he tried to remember, he became distressed, unconsciously wagging his head from side to side.

"All right, Rob. I think that's enough for today. How do you feel?"

"Not too good," he sighed.

"All right. You can relax now. Just close your eyes and breathe slowly. Is prot there with you?"

"Yes, but he doesn't want to be bothered. He says he's thinking."

"Okay, Rob, that's all for now. Oh—one more thing: I'd like to put you under hypnosis next time. Would that be all right with you?"

His pupils seemed to visibly shrink. "Do we have to do that?"

"I think it would help you to get well. You want to get well, don't you?"

"Yes," he said, somewhat mechanically.

"Okay. We'll do an easy test on Tuesday to determine how good a subject you are for the procedure."

"We won't be meeting on Monday?"

"Monday is Labor Day. We'll meet again next Wednesday."

"Oh. Okay." He seemed relieved.

"Thank you for coming in. It was a good session."

"Terrif. So long, doc." On his way out he grabbed a couple of pears and bit into one of them, and I knew that Rob had "retired" for the day.

"Prot?"

"Yeah?"

"Want to go to a picnic on Monday?"

"Will there be fruit?"

"Of course."

"Count me in."

"Good. And I wonder if you'd do me another favor."

He mumbled something in pax-o.

"I've got a patient I'd like you to talk to." I told him about Michael. He seemed quite interested in the case. "If I let you into Ward Three will you try to help him?"

"Help him commit suicide?"

"No, goddamn it. Help talk him out of it."

"I wouldn't dream of it."

"Why not?"

"It's his life. But I'll tell you what I'll do. I'll find out why he wants to do it and see if we can work something out."

"Thank you. That's all I'm asking. I'll set something up as soon—"

"Time!" prot shrieked. "And someone's wai-ting!"

I thought he meant Rodrigo, who had brought him up, but when I opened the door Betty was there with Kowalski. "Problem in the wards?" I asked them.

"It's Bert."

"Where's everyone else?"

"Most of the doctors have gone home early for the weekend."

"Listen—will you and Roman take prot down to 3B? I want him to talk to Michael. I'll be there shortly."

"Sure."

Prot said, "I know the way."

"I want Betty to see this, too."

He smiled tolerantly. "Okay, coach."

I ran to the stairs and down to the second floor, wondering what could have gone wrong with Bert, who can get along for days or weeks without a fuss before becoming desperately anxious about finding whatever it is he has lost. In this respect he is like the patients suffering from manic depression (bipolar disorder), traveling the mountainous road between indifference and near panic.

Bert has been with us for only a few months, arriving not long after he spent his own surprise birthday party destroying the shrubbery and beating in the neighbor's garage door frantically searching for something. A fine athlete who looks much younger than his forty-eight years, he would seem to be a man who has everything: friends, a job he loves, excellent physical health.

All the likely things were checked out early on, of course—a safety deposit key, a briefcase, his wallet—nothing of any importance seemed to be missing. Nor did it seem to be anything so obvious as a loss of youth (his hair was still thick and flaming red), of money or religious faith, or of a family member, or even the respect of his coworkers, factors that sometimes play a role in one's state of well-being. The only clue we had was a closet full of dolls his mother had discovered when she paid him an earlier visit. But even that led nowhere.

On this particular occasion Bert was accosting everyone he encountered, loudly demanding that they empty their pockets and subject themselves to a "body search." I tried unsuccessfully to calm him down, but, as usual, ended up ordering a shot of Thorazine.

While I was helping get him back to his room, one of the nurses came running up, out of breath. "Dr. Brewer! Dr. Brewer! Betty needs you upstairs right away!"

"Where—Ward Four?"

"No! Ward Three! It's prot!" My first thought was: Damn! What's he done to Michael?

I signaled for someone to take over. "What happened?" I asked the nurse as we ran for the stairs. Suddenly I remembered prot's comment about Robert's attempt to drown himself in 1985: *He has that right, doesn't he?* I had made a stupid, amateurish, tactical mistake. Prot might well have agreed with Michael's desire to end his life and tried to help him.

"It's the autistic patients," she puffed. "Something's happened to them!"

"What? What's happened to them?" But we were already banging into 3B and there was no need for further explanation. In my thirty-two years of practice I have seen some terrible and some wonderful things. Nothing could match what we found there that afternoon.

Prot was sitting on a stool facing one of the autists. It was Jerry, the matchstick engineer, who had not said six words of his own since he arrived at the hospital some three years earlier. Prot was squeezing and stroking one of his hands in a warm and tender way, as if caressing a bird.

Jerry, who had not looked anyone in the eye since he was an infant, was gazing into prot's. And he was speaking! Not loudly or frenetically, but quietly, almost in a whisper.

Betty was off to one side, smiling in her teary way. We edged toward her. Jerry was telling prot about his childhood, about certain things he liked to do, about his favorite foods, his love for architectural structures. Prot listened intently, nodding occasionally. After a while he squeezed Jerry's hand one last time and let it go. At that instant, poor Jerry's eyes wandered to the walls, to the furniture, anywhere but to the people in the room. Finally he got up and went back to working on his latest model, a space shuttle on its launch pad. In short, he reverted immediately to his usual state of being, the only existence he had known for the twenty-one years of his pathetic life. The whole episode had lasted only a few minutes.

Betty, still teary-eyed, said, "He did it for three of the others, too."

Prot turned to me. "Gene, gene, gene, where the mischief 'ave you been?"

"How did you do that?"

"I've told you before, doc. You just have to give them your undivided attention. The rest is easy." With that, he headed for the stairs, Kowalski trotting along behind.

"And that's only half of it," Betty said, blowing her nose.

"What's the other half?"

"I think Michael is cured!"

"Cured? C'mon, Betty, you know it doesn't work that way."

"I know it doesn't. But I think this time it did."

"What did prot say to him?"

"Well, you know Michael has always held himself re-sponsible for the death of anyone he has ever had any direct contact with?"

"Yes."

"Prot found a way out for him."

"A way out? What way out?"

"He suggested that Michael become an EMS technician."

"Huh? How would that solve his problem?"

"Don't you see? He can make up for any deaths he has caused by saving other people's lives. He neutralizes his mistakes, so to speak, one at a time. It's perfectly logical. At least it is to Michael. And prot."

"Is Mike in his room now? I'd like to see him for a minute."

"I sent him to the library with Ozzie in Security. He couldn't wait to get hold of a manual on emergency med-ical procedures. You'll see. He's a totally different person!"

A great many thoughts raced around my head as I stared out the window of the train to Connecticut. I was thrilled that prot had apparently been able to do something for Michael that I, in several months of therapy, had not. And his interaction with the autists was something I would never forget. (Before leaving my office I called Villers, Jerry's staff physician, and told him as calmly as I could manage what had happened. His only comment was an unemotional "Zat is so?")

As I gazed at the houses and lawns flying by I wondered whether psychoanalysis had somehow gotten on the wrong track. Why couldn't we see things as clearly as prot seemed to be able to? Was there some simple shortcut to a person's psyche if we only knew how to find it? A way to peel back the layers of the soul and put our hands on its core, to massage it like a stopped heart and get it going again?

I recalled Rob's telling me about his nights in the backyard with his binoculars, his father's arm around his shoulder, both of them gazing into the heavens, the dog sniffing around the fence. If I tried hard enough could I become a part of that scene, feel what he must have felt?

I blamed my father for my loneliness as a child. As our town's only doctor, he commanded a great deal of respect, and this aura seemed to transfer to me as well. The other boys treated me as if I were somehow different, and I had a hard time making friends even though I desperately wanted to be one of them. As a result I became somewhat introverted, a characteristic I retain to this day, unfortunately. If it hadn't been for Karen living right next door I might have ended up a basket case.

I frankly envied Rob his relationship with his father and with his dog. I, too, wanted a dog. My father wouldn't hear of it. He didn't like dogs. I think he may have been afraid of them.

On the other hand, if he or I had been different, or if he had lived longer, perhaps I wouldn't have become a psychiatrist. As Goldfarb is fond of saying, "If my grandmother had wheels, she'd be a wagon." As I stared into the hazy sunlight trying to make some sense of Robert/prot's life, I suddenly thought of Cassandra, our resident seer. Could *she* tell me what would happen if prot left or, for that matter, whether he was, in fact, departing on the twentieth?

I didn't feel much like going in on Saturday, but Dustin's parents had requested a meeting with me and it was the only time I could manage. I found them waiting in the lounge. We chatted for a few minutes about the weather, the hospital food, the worn spots in the carpet. I had met them before, of course. They seemed a genial couple willing to try to help their son in any way possible, visiting him often and assuring me we had their complete confidence and full support.

They had requested the meeting to discuss Dustin's progress. I told them frankly that there hadn't been much as yet, but we were thinking about trying some of the newer experimental drugs. As I talked with these gentle people, I found myself contemplating the possibility that despite their almost obsequious behavior, they might have abused Dustin in some way. A similar case came to mind involving a beloved minister and his wife who had, together, beaten their small boy to death. No one in the congregation seemed to have noticed the bruises and contusions, or they chose to ignore them. Could Dustin's be a similar case? Was he harboring injuries we hadn't yet been able to detect, presenting us with cryptic hints to the underlying cause of his problem?

Child molestation takes many forms. It can be sexual, or involve other types of physical or mental abuse. Because of the child's fear and reluctance to tell anyone else, it is one of the most difficult aberrations to track down. A visit to a doctor will sometimes turn up evidence for such maltreatment (though physicians, too, are sometimes reticent about acting in such instances). But Dustin's medical records indicated no such problem, and it wasn't until he was in high school that he suddenly "snapped." Why it happened then is a mystery, as is the case, unfortunately, for many of our patients.

SESSION TWENTY-THREE

I was gripped, as usual, by a strong sense of déjà vu as Karen and I waited for everyone to show up on a sunny, though relatively cool, Labor Day. It was here, five years ago, that I first became aware of the turmoil roiling deep inside prot's (Robert's) mind, and that I caught a glimpse of his ability to influence people's lives, not only those of the patients but members of my own family as well.

Shasta and Oxeye, the dalmatians, sniffed about the yard, keeping an eye on the front gate as well as the picnic table. They were well aware that visitors were on their way.

Only half the family would be coming to this, the last cookout of the summer. Our oldest son Fred was on location shooting a film musical (he had a part in the chorus), and Jennifer, the internist, was unable to get away from the clinic in San Francisco. In fact, we hadn't seen either of them for several months. One by one, it appears, your children separate the ties and slip away. At moments like this I begin to feel older and older, less and less relevant, as the drumbeat of time grows ever louder and harder to ignore. Though still (barely) in my fifties, I find myself wondering whether retirement might not be preferable to running down like an old grandfather clock.

Karen keeps asking me when I'm going to put away my yellow pad, and sometimes I think it would be quite wonderful to spend my days wandering leisurely around the wards, chatting with the patients, getting to know them intimately as prot does, a knack that Will, and a few of the nurses, seem to have been born with. A busman's retirement, to be sure, but I know one or two drivers who love to spend their holidays riding around the country seeing things they had missed before. And no more cottage cheese!

Abigail and her husband Steve and the kids were the first to arrive. Abby greeted me warmly. As both of us have grown older she has begun to understand that I did my best as a father, as I, in turn, have come to grips with my own father's shortcomings. We all make mistakes, we never get it right, as she is learning for herself, which (as prot pointed out) is probably the only way any of us ever really learn anything.

Abby, perhaps sensing an ally in our alien visitor, took the opportunity, which she hadn't done in years, to ask me whether I realized yet that animal experimentation was "the most costly mistake in the history of medical science. Not that some good hasn't come of it," she went on before I could respond, "as there would be for almost any piss-ass approach to scientific problems. But we have to ask how much farther we might have progressed if better methodologies had been developed decades ago."

I reminded my daughter, the radical, that she might get farther with her case if she cleaned up her language a little, and if the animal-rights people would stop breaking into laboratories and terrorizing researchers.

"Oh, Dad, you're so fucking *establishment*. As if property and what you call 'bad language' were more important than the animals you kill every day. They called the war (she meant Vietnam) protesters terrorists, too, remember? Now we know that was just bullshit. They were *right* and everybody knows it. It's exactly the same now with the animal-rights movement. Fortunately," she added, only half jokingly, "all you old farts will peter out someday and things will change. The younger guys are beginning to see the folly of animal research." Then she smiled and kissed me on the cheek. Happily, all our arguments end this way.

My astronomer son-in-law Steve knew all about Charlie Flynn's interview with prot, and he reported that his colleague was busy searching the skies with renewed vigor for evidence of inhabited planets. Over the past few years Flynn has received a number of prestigious awards for his "discoveries" of several previously unknown worlds, including Noll and Flor and Tersipion, all of which were brought to his attention by prot in 1990. He and some of his colleagues were also working with officials at the State Department in hopes of visiting Libya or, at a minimum, of arranging to import as much excrement as possible from a certain spider indigenous to that country. And he had put all his graduate students to work shining lights into mirrors, hoping they would skip across the laboratory at superlight speeds, so far without success. "Ah love it," Steve drawled. "It's just like bein' in a sci-fi novel."

My grandsons Rain and Star, ages eleven and nine respectively, had a good time that day, primarily because of the dogs, I suppose, with whom they are great friends. As soon as they arrived the great Frisbee chase began, the boys' shoulder-length hair flying out behind them like little flags. Shasta Daisy, now thirteen, hard of hearing and somewhat arthritic, became a puppy again in the excitement of the chase.

Betty and her husband Walt and the triplets arrived a little later with Giselle and prot, whom Shasta recognized at once from the similar visit five years earlier. Oxeye approached him as well, though somewhat more cautiously. Perhaps he instinctively realized this was not Robert, the silent companion of his puppyhood (I had brought Oxie to the catatonic ward in a feeble attempt to get Rob to relate to him). In any case, the dogs rarely left his side all afternoon.

Finally came Will, who brought his girlfriend Dawn. Will had just finished his summer stint at MPI, disappointed that he had not been able to decipher Dustin's secret code. He was sure it had something to do with the "cigar" pantomime, but he couldn't figure out what. He came to relax on this Labor Day, his final free day before classes began, but he was also hoping to speak with prot about how he might be able to communicate with Dustin.

Nothing extraordinary happened for most of the afternoon, and we all enjoyed a terrific backyard picnic. When that was over, and everyone was sitting around talking, I took prot aside and asked him how Robert was feeling.

"He seems to be doing okay, gino. It must be your chairside manner."

"Thank you. Which reminds me—there's something I need to ask you while you're here."

"Ask away."

"In our last session, Robert called his father his 'friend and protector.' Do you know what he meant by that?"

"I never met his father. I didn't know Rob when his father was alive."

"I know. I just thought he might have mentioned something about him to you." I reached into my pocket and pulled out the whistle I had used to bring Robert forward during session twenty. "Remember this?"

"Not the briar patch! Oh, dear! Oh, dear! Anything but the briar patch!" Prot threw up his hands in mock dismay, though I could tell he had been expecting this. Everyone else had been warned, and all the adults present, particularly Giselle, were glancing somewhat nervously in our direction. I winked at her reassuringly. The boys, even little Huey, Louie, and Dewey, were also sitting still, the dogs at their feet. It was suddenly very quiet.

I had no idea whether it would work here, whether Robert was ready to make an appearance outside the relative security of my examining room. As soon as I touched the whistle to my lips, his head dropped for a moment, then raised again. I didn't even have to blow it.

"Hello, Dr. Brewer," he said. His eyes jerked around like a pair of frightened butterflies. "Where am I?" He removed prot's dark glasses so he could see better.

"You are at my home in Connecticut. Your second safe haven. Come on. I'll introduce you to everyone."

But before I could do that, Oxeye came running toward us, his tail flapping. He jumped up and began licking Robert's face (we were sitting in lawn chairs at the back of the yard). Obviously he recognized his former companion and was very glad to see him. Shasta, on the other hand, was less demonstrative. She had met Robert only once, when he freaked out at the sight of our lawn sprinkler.

For his part, Rob was overjoyed to see Oxie again, and he hugged him for several minutes. "I've missed you!" he exclaimed. The dog wagged his tail from ear to ear before running joyfully all over the yard, making several close passes at Rob, as happy dalmatians will do. Later, Rob asked me whether we would keep his dog for him "a little longer." I assured him that we would be happy to do so, pleased that his outlook had become so positive.

Out of the confines of the hospital and prot's influence, Robert showed a side of himself I had not seen before. He was a courteous, kind, soft-spoken man who loved children, and he demonstrated for the boys a number of wrestling holds before joining in on a rip-roaring Frisbee chase with all five, and the dogs as well. If he had not been a mental patient, one would never have suspected there were demons gnawing and scratching just beneath his placid exterior.

Steve tried to engage him in a conversation about the heavens at one point, but gave up when it became apparent that Robert had only a cursory knowledge of the skies— the names of the planets and a few constellations. On the other hand, they both enjoyed comparing notes on their favorite college and professional football teams, though Robert was virtually unaware of developments in that sport since the mid-eighties.

But it was Giselle who occupied most of his time.

Though she seemed to resent his presence at first, she was soon chatting quietly with him about her background and his (both came from small towns), and I certainly didn't discourage this. The more comfortable Rob became with these new and unfamiliar surroundings, the more he was likely to trust us and the better the prognosis. As I watched them I wondered whether it would be Robert or prot who would be returning to the hospital with Betty and her family.

But Rob didn't last out the afternoon. When he went into the house to use the bathroom it was prot who came out, dark glasses and all. Whether the interior had reminded him of that fateful day in 1985 I wasn't sure, but I made no attempt to recall his alter ego. I was delighted he had made an appearance at all.

When Will discovered that prot had returned he immediately pressed him about Dustin's "secret code."

"You mean you haven't worked that out yet? About the carrot and all? Ehhhh"—*chomp, chomp, chomp*—"what's up, doc?"

"Carrot?" Will stammered. "I thought it was a cigar."

"Why would he be munching a cigar?"

"Well—okay—what does the carrot mean?"

"You're smarter than your father. You figure it out."

Some of the others wanted to talk to prot as well. Steve pumped him about his own specialty, the formation of stars, and Giselle tried to get him to "speak" with Shasta, to find out whether he could learn anything about her background. Abby wanted to know how to get more people to sympathize with the plight of animals the world over. "Don't stifle your children's natural feelings toward them," he advised her. And even *they* were grilling him, wanting to know more about what life was like on K-PAX. Star, for example, wondered whether K-PAX was as pretty as the Earth.

Prot's eyes seemed to glaze over. "You can't imagine how beautiful it is," he murmured. "The sky changes from deep red to bright blue and back again, depending on which sun the illuminated side is facing. Rocks, fields of grains, faces— everything—glow in the radiant energy of the suns. And it's so quiet you can hear korms flying and other beings breathing far off in the distance. . . ."

I never did get a chance to ask him any of the host of questions I had been saving for him myself. That, like so many other matters, would have to wait for another time.

Although I had already brought Robert forth after hypnotizing prot, for certain technical reasons I wanted to bypass the latter and deal directly with Rob. I had scheduled Robert's hypnosis-susceptibility (Stanford) test for early Tuesday morning, but was not surprised that it was prot who showed up. I took the opportunity to ask him, with no little trepidation, about my family and how they were doing (it was prot who put me on to Will's drug problem five years earlier).

"Your wife makes a great fruit salad," he said, stuffing his mouth to the brim with raspberries.

As patiently as I could manage, "Anything else?"

He squished the berries around in his mouth; a little stream of blood-red juice ran down his chin. "Abby seems to be one of the few human beings who understand what it will take to save the EARTH from yourselves. Of course she has some rough edges. . . ." He grinned wryly and a masticated berry tumbled from his mouth. "I like that."

"Dammit, prot, what about Will?"

"What about him?"

"Is he taking any drugs?"

"Only sex and caffeine. You humans never cease trying to find something to fulfill your boring lives, do you?"

"It may surprise you to learn, my friend, that there's no one on Earth more human than yourself."

"No need for insults, gino."

I laughed at that, perhaps out of relief. "So you think Will is doing all right, then?"

"He'll be a great doctor, *mon ami*."

"Thank you. I'm very happy to hear that."

"Anytime."

I could see from the lopsided grin that he still wasn't going to tell me when he would be leaving or who he planned to take with him. However, something else had occurred to me as I was driving in that morning. "Prot?"

"Yeth thir?" in his Daffy Duck voice. I thought: He's been hanging around Milton too long.

"Betty told me she saw you in the quiet room reading *K-PAX*."

"I was curious."

"Did you find any inaccuracies in it?"

"Only your absurd speculation that I am merely a figment of robert's imagination."

"That brings up an interesting question I've been meaning to ask you: How come I've never seen you and Robert at the same time?"

He slapped his forehead. "Gene, gene, gene. Have you ever seen me and the world trade center at the same time?"

"No."

"Then I presume you think the world trade center doesn't exist?"

"You know, there's a better way to conclusively prove or disprove that you and Robert are the same person. Will you give us a blood sample?"

"You already sampled it when I was here the first time, remember?"

"Unfortunately, it was accidentally discarded. May we have a little more?"

"There are no accidents, my friend. But why not? I've got plenty."

"I'll set it up with Dr. Chakraborty for later this week, okay?"

"Hokay, joe."

"Now—I need to speak to Robert for a while. Will you tell him, please?"

"Tell him what, Dr. Brewer?"

"Oh, hello, Robert. How are you feeling?"

"All right, I guess."

"Good. I brought you here to see how good a candidate you would be for hypnosis, remember?"

"I remember."

"All right. Just relax for a moment." I explained the procedure to him. He listened carefully, nodded at the appropriate times, and we began.

The procedure took almost an hour. Robert was tested for a number of simple responses to hypnotic suggestion, such as arm immobilization, verbal inhibition, etc. Whereas prot had obtained a perfect score of twelve on the same test, I was surprised to find that Robert did very poorly with a four, considerably below average. I wondered whether this represented a genuine lack of aptitude or he was fighting it. Having no good alternative, I decided to go ahead with the next session as planned, though with less confidence than I would have liked.

If Robert was going to get well there would have to be better reasons for him to stay out of his protective shell than to retreat into it. Thus, I wanted and needed Giselle's help in his treatment, despite her stronger feelings for prot. She was strategically placed to act as a sort of liaison between Rob and the world. I asked her, over lunch, what she thought of him.

"He's okay. A nice enough guy. In fact, I like him."

"I'm glad to hear that. Giselle, I have to ask you a favor. Robert is struggling to maintain his identity, even in my examining room. He made a brief appearance yesterday at my home, but that's about it. As far as I know he's never shown up in the wards. Have you ever seen him in Two?"

"No, I haven't."

"Here's the thing. Somehow fate has placed you in a unique position to help him. Will you try to do that? As a favor to me as well as him? I'll give you free access to him—no more time limits."

"Why not just whistle him out like you did before?"

"That was a special occasion. I don't want to shock him by bringing him out in the wards before he's ready."

"What can I do?"

115

"What I *don't* want you to do is to try to entice Rob to come forward. What I'd like you to do is to make him feel comfortable so he'll *stay* out when he does show up."

Her eyebrows lifted. "How do I do that?"

"Just be nice to him. As nice as possible. Talk to him. Find out what he's interested in. Play games with him. Read to him. Anything you can think of to keep him around. I want him to like you. I want him to depend on you. I want you to be there for him." I almost said, "Try to love him"— but that was asking a bit too much. "Are you up to such a challenge?"

She smiled, I think, though it was hard to tell with her mouth stuffed with food. "It's the least I can do," she mumbled, "for letting me be with prot so much of the time."

"Good." I scraped my plate, wishing as usual that there were more cottage cheese. "Now—what else is happening?"

"Well, there's an anthropologist and a chemist coming later this week. To talk to prot, I mean."

"What do they want?"

"I think the anthropologist wants to know about the progenitors of the 'dremer' species on K-PAX, maybe get some idea of what our own forefathers might have been like. The chemist wants to ask him about the flora of the Amazonian rain forest, which he's been studying for twenty years or so. He wants to know where to look for drugs to treat AIDS and various forms of cancer and so on."

"Let me know what he tells them, if anything. Anybody else lined up?"

"A cetologist is coming next week. He wants prot to talk to a dolphin he knows."

"He's bringing a dolphin?"

"He's got a big tank that he pulls around to fairs and shopping malls. He's going to bring it and the dolphin to the front of the hospital so that prot can talk to him."

"Good grief—what next?"

"As prot might say, 'Anything is possible.' "

That afternoon I met with several of the faculty in Ward Four, where the psychopathic patients are housed. The reason for this gathering was that a new inmate had been brought in, someone who had planned and carried out a series of murders in all five boroughs of the city. Such patients are usually assigned to Ron Menninger, who specializes in psychopathy, with Carl Thorstein taking the overload.

The entire faculty, except for those unable to make it owing to other commitments, usually shows up for the first "session" with a new resident of Four—not only to help his psychiatrist evaluate his condition and possible course of treatment, but also to assess the potential danger to the rest of the staff and patients.

The new inmate, wearing bright orange-plastic shackles, was brought in by two of the security guards and asked to sit at the end of the long table. Ordinarily I'm not surprised by the general appearance of a psychopathic patient because there is no mold into which such a person fits. A "path" can be young or old, hardened or timid. He can look like a derelict or the boy next door. But I winced when this cold-blooded killer was brought in. I had been informed, of course, that she was a female Caucasian, but it was hard to imagine, even with decades of experience, that such a beautiful woman could be guilty of committing the crimes alleged to her. Yet she had been tried, found not responsible by reason of insanity, and sent to MPI for killing seven young men in various parts of the city.

Serial killings, indeed most murders, are usually committed by men. Whether this has anything to do with the male (or female) psyche, or is merely a matter of opportunity, is not at all clear. Psychopathy itself is a difficult affliction to understand. As with many mental illnesses, there seems to be a genetic defect often leading to an underarousal of the autonomic nervous system. Persons harboring this defect, for example, exhibit little anxiety when confronted with a potentially dangerous situation. In fact, they seem to enjoy it.

In addition, psychopaths are often quite impulsive, acting mainly on feelings of the moment, seeking short-lived thrills without regard to the long-term consequences. They are usually sociopathic as well, caring little for the feelings of others and evincing little regard for what other people may think of them.

On the other hand, they are often superficially charming, making it very difficult for potential victims to spot danger in ordinary interactions with them. How does one recognize that "the nice boy (or girl) next door" can be as deadly as an anaconda?

But back to our patient. The woman, only twenty-three, was thought to have murdered seven young men, perhaps as many as nine, all from outlying towns, who had come to the big city for a good time on a Saturday night. All seven were found in deserted areas, unclad from the waist down, and penectomized. She was apprehended only when she picked up a police decoy, who barely escaped with his life, not to mention his genitalia.

But charming she was, and lovely as well. She smiled as she gazed into the eyes of every doctor in the room. Her answers to routine questions were frank, sometimes humorous, not the slightest bit antisocial. And I thought: Can we ever really know a person, even one who is perfectly sane? I knew that Ron was in for a very interesting experience. Nevertheless, I didn't envy him in the slightest, even when she wet her lips and winked at me as if to say, "Let's have some fun."

When I got back to my office I perused the "poop sheet" on our newest patient, whom I will call Charlotte. One by one her victims had disappeared and were never heard from again. The reason it took the police so long to find her was that young men come to town every weekend to pick up girls, and even under the best of circumstances it is virtually impossible to find an unknown killer in a city full of people. Probably no one would even take notice of a young couple leaving the bar or restaurant where they met, perhaps arm in arm, smiling warmly, Mr. Fly eagerly accompanying Ms. Spider to her web.

Perhaps that's why I have trouble sympathizing with spiders, even when they get trapped in a sink.

Before leaving for the day I sought out Cassandra. I found her sitting on the weathered bench under "Adonis in the Garden of Eden," her raven-black hair shining in the sun, gazing at the cloudless sky from which she gets her inspiration, or so she claims. Knowing she ignores any attempt to interrupt her, I waited.

When she finally turned her attention away from the heavens I cautiously approached her. She seemed in a pleasant enough mood, and we chatted for a while about the hot weather. She predicted more of the same. I said, "That's not what I wanted to ask you about."

"Why not? Everyone else does."

"Cassandra, I wonder if you could help me with something."

"It won't be the Mets."

"No, not that. I need to know how long prot is going to be around. Can you tell me anything about when he'll be leaving us?"

"If you're planning a trip to K-PAX, don't pack your bags yet."

"You mean it will be a while before he goes?"

"When he's finished what he came to do, he'll leave. That will take some time."

"May I ask you—did you get this information from prot himself?"

She looked annoyed, but admitted she had talked with him.

"Anything else you can tell me about your conversation with prot?"

With a hint of amusement now: "I asked if he would take me with him."

"What did he say?"

"He told me I was one of those being considered."

"Really? Do you know who else is on the list?"

She tapped her head with a forefinger. "He said you would ask me that."

"Do you know the answer?"

"Yes."

"Who are they?"

"Anyone who wants to go."

But not everyone on the list will be selected, I thought dismally. A lot of them are going to be very disappointed. "All right. Thank you, Cassie."

"Don't you want to know who's going to win the World Series?"

"Who?"

"The Braves."

I almost blurted out, "You're crazy!"

SESSION TWENTY-FOUR

Whenever I experience a difficult patient making a first appearance in Ward Four, I always pay a visit to Ward One to try to recapture my optimism, and I did so the morning after meeting Charlotte. I encountered Rudolph in the exercise room practicing what appeared to be very novel ballet stances and moves. It reminded me of the contortionists who used to appear on *The Ed Sullivan Show*. I asked him how he was doing. To my surprise he confessed that he had a long way to go. I wasn't sure whether he meant his treatment program or his perfection of ballet technique, but I could see that he wouldn't be with us much longer.

I found Michael in the quiet room behind a book of poetry. I asked him what he was reading.

"Oh, just some Keats and Shelley and Wordsworth and those guys. An anthology. I've missed out on so much of my life. When I was in high school I wanted to be an English teacher."

"Still can be."

"Maybe. Right now I just want to balance the ledger."

"Have you looked into any EMS training programs?"

"I've already signed up for one. Starts October third." He glanced at me hopefully.

"I think you'll make it. I'll take a look at my schedule and see if we can work in a wrap-up session sometime soon."

On the way back to my office I stopped briefly in Ward Two, where my balloon of optimism began to deflate with a pronounced hiss. Bert was crashing through the lounge lifting cushions, stomping on the carpet, peering behind drapes and chairs. How sad he seemed, focused on his impossible quest like some latter-day Don Quixote.

But was Bert's case any more tragic than that of Jackie, who would always be a child? Or Russell, so focused on the Bible that he never learned how to live? Or Lou or Manuel or Dustin? Or, for that matter, some of our faculty and staff? Or millions of others who stumble about the world looking for what may not be there? Who set impossible goals for themselves and never attain them?

Milton, perhaps noticing my sudden melancholy, held forth with: "Man went to the doctor. Said he had chest pains and wanted an electrocardiogram. Doctor gave him one and told him there was nothing wrong with his heart. Came in every few months. Same result. Outlived three doctors. Finally, when he was ninety-two, there was a change in his EKG pattern. He looked the guy straight in the eye and said, 'Ha! I told you so!' "

Now in his fifties, Milton fully understands the sadness of life and tries vainly to cheer up everyone he sees. Unfortunately, he has never been able to alleviate his own suffering. He lost his entire family—father, mother, brothers, a sister, grandmother, several aunts and uncles and cousins, in the Holocaust. Only he escaped, protected from harm by a total stranger, a gentile who took the baby at the pleadings of his mother and pretended it was her own.

But is his story any sadder than that of Frankie, a woman unable to form human relationships of any kind? Not a sociopath like Charlotte, nor an autist like Jerry and the others, but someone who is indifferent toward affection, a patient who is pathologically unable to love or be loved—what could be sadder than that?

Villers was leaving the dining room as I was coming in. I waved at him as he passed by but he didn't see me. He seemed distracted, deep in thought, conjuring up some new money-making scheme, I assumed.

Menninger joined me instead, and I asked him about his new patient. "She's as cold as they come," he told me, "a female Hannibal Lecter. You should read her detailed history."

"I think I'll pass on that."

But Ron was enjoying himself. He loves to play with fire. "When she was five, she killed a puppy. You know how she did it?"

"No."

"She baked it in the oven."

"Did she get any treatment?"

"Nope. Claimed she didn't know the pup was in there."

"And it went downhill from there."

"Way down."

I slowly chewed up the last of the crackers. "I'm not sure I want to hear the rest."

"I'll give you the low point. After several more practice runs with neighborhood pets, including a horse she stabbed to death, she killed the boy next door when she was sixteen."

"How did she get by with it?"

"She didn't. She spent some time in a reform school and then was transferred to a mental institution when she attacked one of the guards. You don't want to know what she did to him. She managed to escape from that place and was never heard from again."

"How old was she then?"

"Twenty. She was arrested a year later."

"You mean she killed those seven or eight guys in one year?"

"And that's not the worst of it. When she killed the neighbor kid?"

"Yes?"

"She left him lying in the backyard and went to a movie. After that, she slept like a baby, according to her parents."

"I'd keep an eye on her if I were you."

His eyes lit up. "Don't worry. But she's an amazing case, don't you think? I've never met anyone like her." He seemed beside himself, eager for his first session with Charlotte.

"Just be careful. She's no Sunday-school teacher."

"Wouldn't matter if she were."

"Why not?"

"Some of the most violent people in the world are Sunday-school teachers."

While waiting for Robert/prot to come in for his twenty-fourth session I jotted down on a yellow pad some of the missing pieces of the puzzle I hoped to obtain from Rob, paramount of which was the question of who had fathered Sarah's child, and what, if anything, did this have to do with Rob's mental problems? Why did he call his father his "protector"? What happened when he was five years old that he couldn't, or wouldn't, remember? None of this was going to be easy for Rob to deal with, but I was pretty sure the seeds of his trauma had begun to germinate during that early period in his troubled life, as my perceptive wife had suggested.

There was another, quite unforeseen, difficulty as well. Based on the results of the Stanford test, it appeared that Robert was trying hard to resist being hypnotized. Was he beginning to have second thoughts about cooperating with me and getting to the bottom of the quagmire he had been treading most of his life? I decided to approach his child-hood only indirectly for the time being.

From his history I knew approximately when Sarah must've become pregnant, so I had some idea of when she told him about it. I tried to imagine what he must have felt upon hearing this news, and I was still staring into empty space when someone tapped on the door.

"Hi, Dr. Brewer."

"Hello, Rob. How are you feeling?"

He shrugged.

"Do you remember coming here from Ward Two?"

"No."

"What's the last thing you remember?"

"I was being tested to see whether I could be hypnotized."

"Well, you passed."

His shoulders slumped.

"And you know that in this setting there's no danger, nothing to worry about, right? Are you ready to try it?"

"I guess."

"Okay, sit down and relax. Good. Now focus your attention on that little spot on the wall behind me."

He pretended not to see it. After a moment, however, he complied.

"That's it. Just relax. Good. Good. Now I'm going to count from one to five. You will begin to feel drowsy on one, your eyelids will become heavier and heavier as the numbers increase, and by the time I get to five you will be asleep, but you will be able to hear everything I say. Do you understand?"

"Yes."

"Good. Now—let your arms drop. . . ." Rob's arms fell heavily to his sides and his eyes closed tightly. He began to snore softly. Obviously he was faking it. "Okay, Rob, open your eyes."

His eyes popped open. "Is it over already?"

"Rob, you'll have to do better than that. Are you afraid of the procedure?"

"No, not exactly."

"Good. Now let's try again. Are you comfortable?"

"Yes."

"All right. Now let yourself relax completely. Let all your muscles go limp and just relax. That's it. Good. Now find the spot on the wall. Good. Just relax. One . . . you're beginning to feel drowsy. Two . . . your eyelids are getting heavy. . . ." Robert stared at the white dot. He was still resisting, apparently caught between fear and suspicion. On three his eyelids began to flutter, and he fought to keep them open. By the count of five they were closed and his chin had dropped onto his chest. "Rob? Can you hear me?"

"Yes."

"Good. Now lift your head and open your eyes."

He complied. I checked his pulse and coughed loudly. There was no reaction.

"How do you feel?"

"Okay."

"Good. All right, Rob, we're going to go back in time now. Imagine the pages of a calendar turning backward, backward, backward. You are slowly becoming younger. Younger and younger. You are thirty, twenty-five, twenty. Now you're a senior in high school. It's March 1975. Almost spring. You have a date with your girlfriend Sally. You're picking her up now. Where are you going?"

"We're going to a movie."

"What movie are you going to?"

"*Jaws.*"

"Okay. What is Sally wearing?"

"She's wearing her yellow coat and scarf."

"It's cold outside?"

"Not too cold. Her coat is open. She has on a white blouse and a blue skirt."

"Are you driving or walking?"

"Walking. I don't have a car."

"All right. You're at the theater. You're going in. What happens next?"

"I'm buying some popcorn. Sally loves popcorn."

"You don't like it?"

"I'll have a little of hers. I don't have any more money."

"Okay. There's Robert Shaw being eaten by the shark. Now the movie is over and you're leaving the theater. Where are you going now?"

"We're going back to Sally's house. She wants to talk."

"Do you know what she wants to talk about?"

"No. She won't tell me till we get to the house."

"All right, you're back at Sally's house. What do you see?"

Robert seemed to become edgy. "It—it's a big white house with dormers in the roof. We're going to sit on the porch and talk for a while. In one of the swings."

"What is Sally saying to you?"

"Her head is on my shoulder. Her hair is soft. I can smell her shampoo. She tells me she is pregnant."

"How does she know that?"

"She has missed two periods."

"Are you the father?"

"No. We've never done anything."

"You've never had a sexual relationship with Sally?"

His fists clenched. "No."

"Do you know who the father is?"

"No."

"Sally won't tell you?"

"I never asked her."

"Why not?"

"If she wanted me to know, she'd tell me."

"All right. What are you going to do about it?"

"That's what she wants to talk about."

"What does *she* think you ought to do?"

"She wants to get married. Only—"

"Only what?"

"Only she knows I want to go to college."

"How do *you* feel about it?"

"I want to get married, too."

"And give up your career?"

"I don't have much choice."

"But you're not the father."

"It doesn't matter. I love her."

"So you told her you would marry her?"

"Yes."

"What's happening now?"

"She's kissing me."

"Do you like it when she kisses you?"

"Yes." His reply sounded strangely matter-of-fact.

"Has she ever kissed you before?"

"Yes."

"But it never led to anything further?"

"No."

"Why not?"

"I don't know."

"All right. What's happening now?"

"We're going inside."

"It's too cold to stay on the porch?"

"No. She wants to go up to her room."

"Is she ill?"

"No. She wants me to go, too."

"Tell me what you see."

"We're going up the stairs. Trying to be real quiet because they squeak. It's dark except for a hall light. Everyone else has gone to bed."

"Go on."

"We're tiptoeing down the hallway. It's still squeaking. We're going into Sally's room. She's closing the door. I hear it lock. We're taking off our coats."

"Go on."

"We're hugging and kissing some more. She is pressing herself against me. I'm sorry. I can't help it. I put my hands under her skirt and lift it up."

"Go on, Rob. What's happening now?"

"We move toward the bed. Sally falls down on it. I'm on top of her. No! Please! I don't want to do this!"

"Why not? Why don't you want to have sex with Sally?"

"It's a terrible thing to do! I have to go to sleep now."

"It's all right, Rob. It's over. It's all over. What's happening now?"

"I'm getting dressed."

"How do you feel?"

"I don't know. Better, I guess."

"What is Sally doing?"

"She is just lying there watching me button my shirt. It's dark but I can see her smiling."

"Go on."

"I put my coat on. I have to go."

"Why do you have to go?"

"I told my mother I would be home by eleven-thirty."

"What time is it now?"

"Twenty after eleven."

"What's happening?"

"Sally's getting up and putting her arms around me. She doesn't want me to go. She isn't wearing anything. I try not to look but I can't help it."

"What do you see?"

"She's naked. I can't look. I'm unlocking the door. 'Bye, Sally. I'll see you tomorrow.' I'm tiptoeing along the corridor. Down the stairs. Out the door. I'm running. I run all the way home."

"Is your mother waiting up for you?"

"No. But she hears me come in. She asks if it's me. 'Yes, Mom, it's me.' She wants to know if we had a nice time. 'Yes, Mom, we had a very nice time.' She says good night. I go to my room."

"You're going to bed now?"

"Yes. But I can't sleep."

"Why not?"

"I keep thinking about Sally."

"What do you think about her?"

"How she smells and how she feels and how she tastes."

"Do you like those things?"

"Yes."

"But you can't go all the way?"

"No."

"Rob, can you tell me about anything that happened when you were younger that would make you dislike sex? Something that hurt you, or frightened you?"

No response.

"All right. Now listen carefully. Imagine the calendar again. The pages are turning rapidly, but this time we're coming forward. You're getting older. Twenty, twenty-five, thirty, and still you are getting older. You are thirty-eight years old. It's September 6, 1995, the present time. Do you understand?"

"Yes."

"Good. Now I'm going to count backward from five to one. As I count, you will begin to wake up. When I get to one, you will be fully awake, alert, and feeling fine. Five . . . four . . . three . . . two . . . one—"

"Hello, Dr. Brewer."

"Hello, Rob. How do you feel?"

"You asked me that a minute ago."

"You've been under hypnosis. Do you remember?"

"No."

"All right. May I ask you a few more questions now?"

"Sure." He seemed relieved it was over.

"Good. Rob, you were only five when your father was injured at work, weren't you?"

"Yes."

"Did you visit him in the hospital?"

"They said I was too young. But my mother went to see him every day."

"Who took care of you while your mother was at the hospital?"

"Uncle Dave and Aunt Catherine."

"They came to stay with you?"

He began to fidget. "No. I stayed with them for a while."

"How long?"

He answered slowly, almost in a whisper, "A long time."

"During that time, did anything happen that you want to tell me about?"

"I don't know, gino. I wasn't there."

"Doggone it, prot. Couldn't you have given us a few more minutes? Where's Robert? Is he okay?"

"Bearing up remarkably well, I'd say, under the circumstances."

"What circumstances?"

"Your relentless—how you say eet?—browbeating."

"Is he coming back?"

"Not for a while."

"Prot, what can you tell me about Robert's Uncle Dave and Aunt Catherine?"

"I just told you—I wasn't there."

"He's never told you anything about them?"

"Never heard of any Uncle Dave or Aunt Catherine."

"All right. Have some fruit."

"Thought you'd never ask." He grabbed a cantaloupe and bit into it.

I watched him devour rind, seeds, everything. I was still annoyed with him, but there was no time to waste. "As long as you've barged in—Dr. Villers asked me to sound you out on your TV appearance."

"Sound away."

"Well, are you willing to do it?"

"Who gets the money?"

I thought: Spoken like a true Homo sapiens! "Why, the hospital, I suppose. You don't need money, do you?"

"No being needs money."

"What do you suggest we do with it?"

"I suggest we let the network keep it."

"Otherwise you don't show up?"

"You got it."

"I don't think Klaus is going to like that idea. The main reason you were going on was to raise money for the new wing."

"He'll get used to it."

"Do you want to be on TV?"

"Depends. Why do they want to know what a crazy person has to say?"

"You'd be surprised who goes on talk shows. Actually, they might try to make a fool of you."

"Sounds like fun. I'll be there!"

"All right. I'll tell Villers about your decision."

"Anything else, doc?"

"The trip to the zoo has been scheduled for the fourteenth. That okay with you?"

"Yep. What a place!" He took another huge bite of melon.

I declined to pursue this comment, which could have meant anything. Instead, I seized the opportunity, while I could, to discuss the patients with him. "I saw you talking with Bert this morning."

"How very observant."

"Do you know what he's looking for, by any chance?"

"Sure."

"You do?? What, for God's sake?"

"Ah, gene. Do I have to do *all* your thinking for you?"

"Please, prot. All I'm asking for is a tiny little hint."

"Oh, all right. He's looking for his daughter."

"But he doesn't have a daughter!"

"That's why he can't find her!" He went for the door.

"Wait a minute—where are you going?"

"I don't get paid for overtime."

I called out: "Anything you can do for Frankie?" But he was already gone.

First thing next morning I called Chakraborty and then went looking for prot. On the way to the lounge I ran into Betty and told her what he had said about Bert. Her response was typical: "Prot is really something, isn't he? Maybe you should give him an office and bring all the patients in to see him."

"We've already considered that," I told her resignedly. "But he doesn't want the job."

I found him in the lounge surrounded by his usual entourage, including Russell, who was now insisting that the end of the world was imminent. I asked them to let me speak to our alien friend for a moment. There was a lot of grumbling, but they finally backed away.

"Prot, Dr. Chakraborty is ready to take a little blood from you."

"I shall returrrn," he promised his followers. "Count Drrracula awaits in the crrrypt." Without another word he headed for the door. I started to call out, but I realized he knew exactly where he was going. Suddenly I had the uncomfortable sensation of being surrounded. Someone said, "You're trying to get rid of him, aren't you?"

"Prot? Of course not."

"You're trying to drive him away. Everybody knows that."

"No—I'm trying to get him to stay! For a while, at least. . . ."

"Only as long as it takes to make Robert better. Then you want him to die."

"I don't want anyone to die."

Russell shouted, "If you do not wake up I will come upon you like a thief, and you will not know the moment of my coming!" While everyone was pondering that pronouncement I made a hasty exit.

Giselle came in late that afternoon to report on prot's meeting with the anthropologist and the rain-forest chemist.

"First," I said, "any sign of Robert?"

"Haven't seen him since Labor Day."

"Okay. Go on."

"They turned out to be brother and sister. Hadn't spoken in years. I don't think they like each other much."

"What did he tell them?"

"The chemist seemed suspicious of prot's knowledge and abilities. He demanded to know the names of all the plants that produce natural products that could be used in the fight against AIDS."

"And?"

"Prot just shook his head and said, 'Why must you humans label everything a "fight"? The viruses mean you no malice. They're programmed to survive, like everyone else.'"

"That sounds like him. What happened then?"

"He rephrased the question."

"And did prot give him the information he wanted?"

"No, but he told him where to look for one."

"Where?"

"Somewhere in southwestern Brazil. He even described the plant. It's got big leaves and little yellow flowers. He said the natives call it '*otolo*,' which means 'bitter.' The chemist took this all down, but he still seemed skeptical until prot told him there was a substance good for certain kinds of heart arrhythmias in another plant found in the same region of Brazil. The guy knew all about that drug. In fact, he was one of its co-discoverers. He actually kissed prot's hand. By then his time was up. He took off like a bat."

"What about the anthropologist?"

"Prot told her there were probably several 'missing links' on Earth. She wanted to know where to find them."

"Don't they already know that?"

"Nope. They're not in Africa."

"Where, then?"

"He suggested she go to Mongolia."

"Mongolia? How did they get from there to Africa?"

She gave me a look of prot-like exasperation. "They didn't have cars, Dr. B. They probably walked."

"So I suppose she's off to Mongolia?"

"She leaves next week."

"You realize, of course, that it will be a long time before we know whether prot was right about any of these things."

"No, it won't. We know now."

"How do we know that?"

"What does he have to do to prove to you that he knows what he's talking about? Everything he's told Dr. Flynn so far was right, wasn't it?"

"Maybe. But savants like him only know what is already known. He can't deduce something that nobody knows yet."

"He's not a savant. He's from K-PAX."

We had been through this before. I thanked her for the report and told her I had another favor to ask of her.

"Whatever you say, Dr. B."

"We need to find out whether Bert had a daughter some time in the past. There's no record of it, but maybe it got lost somehow, like Robert's disappearance in '85 went into the books as a suicide."

"I'll get right on it. But first you'll have to give me some information about him."

I handed her a sheet from my yellow pad with all the pertinent data on it. Leaving a piney ghost behind, she was literally off and running. I only hoped she would be half as successful at this task as she had been in tracking down prot's true identity five years earlier.

Right after she left, Klaus Villers came in. I thought he wanted to discuss one of his patients, or perhaps offer some pointed suggestions about one of mine, something he truly loves to do. Instead, he spent fifteen minutes stroking his goatee and telling me the story of Robin Hood. He wanted to know what I thought about the moral implications of that myth for present-day society. I told him I thought that people shouldn't take the law into their own hands, but if they did they should be prepared to pay the consequences. Judging by the inflection of his grunts, I don't think he liked that answer.

SESSION TWENTY-FIVE

The morning before Rob's next session I sat in my office thinking about him and Sally. What could possibly have happened to preclude his having an intimate relationship with his wife-to-be, whom he dearly loved? Did the fact that she was carrying someone else's child have anything to do with it?

Even under the best of circumstances, sex is one of the most difficult things human beings have to deal with. Most of us learn about it piecemeal, on school playgrounds, in the streets, from movies or TV. Some get an introductory course from their father or mother, often in the form of a how-to manual obtained from the local library. Many parents are almost as ignorant about the subject as their children.

The best place to learn about sex, just as it is for every other subject, is the schools. But that idea has come under fire in recent years. The net result of this vacuum is, of course, that teenage pregnancy and venereal diseases are rampant in our society. The kids learn plenty about sex, but they learn it from each other.

My own introduction to this mysterious subject was somewhat less than informed. One hot August afternoon my mother went shopping, leaving Karen and me home alone. We were fourteen or fifteen at the time. We turned on the sprinkler and ran through the spray, back and forth until our shorts and T-shirts were sopping wet, and nearly transparent. Then we "accidentally" bumped into each other, one thing led to another, and—well, it's the old story. Afterward, Karen was sure she was pregnant and I thought I was a rapist. We didn't touch each other again for two years.

Yet, despite all the taboos and other obstacles, most of us manage, through trial and error at least, to find a satisfactory partner and, eventually, to enjoy a more or less successful sex life. Why not Rob?

Later that morning, Will, now back in school but still coming to MPI in his spare time to speak with Dustin and some of the other patients, stopped by my office to see if I wanted to go somewhere for lunch. Though I rarely do so, he and I went out to a nearby restaurant.

Knowing I should eat lightly or fall asleep later on, I decided on a cup of soup and a salad. Will, always a good eater, ordered substantially more.

We chatted for a while. Usually full of restless energy, he seemed withdrawn, nervous. He only picked at his food, claiming he wasn't as hungry as he thought. I may not be the world's greatest father, but even I could tell that something was bothering him, and I suspected what it might be: his girlfriend Dawn was pregnant. My own father, who lived through (and never forgot) the Depression, wouldn't let me leave food on my plate; it's a habit I've never been able to break. I scraped Will's uneaten portions into my empty salad dish.

But his girlfriend wasn't pregnant (as far as I knew). It was worse than that. He was having second thoughts about medical school! Not an unfamiliar topic to me, as I had dealt with similar misgivings thirty-five years earlier. And I had known other students who couldn't take the pressure and finally dropped out. One had committed suicide. A few turned to drugs. This was what was worrying me—Will already had a drug problem.

As I gobbled his lunch, I told him about my own doubts when I was his age, that it was not unusual for a student, or even a doctor, to question his abilities, to feel overwhelmed at times by his awesome responsibility for the lives of his patients. But I also reminded him that it comes with the territory. That he, like all of us, will make mistakes. That no one is perfect and we can only do our best. And in his case, the best was quite good enough. Even prot had said so.

"Prot said that, Pop?"

"He says you're going to be a fine doctor."

"Well, if prot thinks so, maybe I can handle it after all."

Though a bit envious that it had been prot's remark, and none of my own, that had swayed his thoughts and lifted his spirits, I felt relieved that the problem seemed to have been resolved. Now he was hungry. Since I had eaten all of his food, he ordered something more. To keep him company, I had a rich dessert while we discussed Dustin and some of the other patients. Finally he pushed his plate away and took a sip of coffee.

I asked him whether he was finished. He nodded. Since he hadn't eaten everything, I scraped the leftovers onto my dessert plate.

It was a wonderful lunch, the kind I never had a chance to have with my own father. But now I had to go back and try to be a good doctor, despite my own chronic misgivings, on a Friday afternoon and a very full stomach.

"Ah, cherries! No being can eat just one!"

"Prot! Where's Robert?"

Slurp! Munch, munch, munch. "He's taking the day off."

"What do you mean, 'He's taking the day off'?"

"He doesn't want to talk to you today. Give him the weekend. He'll come around." *Crunch, crunch.* "Cherry?"

"No, thanks. Why would he be more willing to talk on Monday than today?"

"He needs to psych himself up for it."

"We're running out of time, prot."

"Haven't we been over this before? Trust me, doc. You can't rush these things. Or would you rather blow your little whistle and put him back the way he was a month ago?"

"It's that bad?"

"You're getting into something he's been trying to run away from for most of his life."

"What is it? Do you know what happened to him?"

"Nope. He never told me."

"Then how do you know—"

"I've been coming here since 1963, remember?"

"So what do we do now?"

"He's almost ready to deal with it. Just give him a little more time."

The only sound on the tape at this point was that of someone's foot tapping, probably my own. "Prot?"

"What you want, *kemo sabe*?"

"Do you think he would feel more comfortable talking to *you* about it first?"

"I don't know. Want me to ask him?"

"Please do."

Prot gazed at the ceiling for a long moment. Unforgivably, I yawned. Ignoring this breach of etiquette, he exclaimed, "Well done, dr. b! He *does* want to tell me first. But he doesn't want *me* to tell *you. He* wants to do it."

"Will he tell you now?"

Prot threw up his hands in a now-familiar gesture of frustration. "Gene, gene, gene! How many times do I have to say this? He wants to do it on Monday. He'll tell me that morning and you in the afternoon. I think it's a pretty good deal, don't you? My advice is to take it."

"I'll take it."

"Good person."

I gazed at him through heavy-lidded eyes as he energetically devoured a couple of pounds of cherries. "Well, we've got some time left," I pointed out. "Maybe *you* would be willing to answer a few questions."

"Anything. Except how to build better bombs or contaminate another PLANET."

I didn't ask him what he figured we'd contaminate it with. Instead, I pulled out my old list of questions, the ones I had brought to the Labor Day picnic but never got a chance to ask him. Of course I had certain ulterior motives for wanting to query him. Maybe he would say something that would give me a better insight into the workings of his (and Robert's) unpredictable mind. "There are a few things you told me during your visit five years ago that I never followed up on. May I do so now?"

"I don't think anything could stop you from asking your relentless questions, gino."

"Thank you. I'll take that as a compliment. By the way, some of these were sent to me by people who read *K-PAX*."

"Hooray for them."

"Ready?"

"Aim. Fire!"

"No need for sarcasm, prot. First, what does 'K-PAX' mean?"

He adopted a stiff, pompous demeanor before proceeding. " 'K' is the highest class of PLANET, the last step in the evolutionary process, the point of perfect peace and stability. 'PAX' means 'a place of purple plains and mountains.' "

"Because of your red and blue suns."

He relaxed again. "Bingo!"

"So 'B-TIK,' what we call Earth, is the second lowest type?"

"Kee-reck. You don't want to know about the 'A' category."

"Why not?"

"Those are WORLDS already destroyed by their own inhabitants. Before that they were 'B's."

"I see. And 'TIK' means—?"

"Beautiful blue water dotted with white clouds."

"Ah, I get it."

"I was beginning to wonder."

"All right. What about Tersipion?"

"Oh, that's what *they* call it. We call it F-SOG."

"Okay. Tell me about some of the other beings you have come across. Like the giant insects on—ah—F-SOG, for example."

"Use your imagination, doc. Anything you can think of, and a lot you can't, exists somewhere. Remember that there are several billion inhabited planets and moons in our GALAXY alone, not to mention a comet or two. Your species can't seem to imagine anything that doesn't work pretty much the same as you do. Your 'experts' are always saying life is impossible somewhere or other because there isn't any water or oxygen or whatever. Wake up and smell the hoobah!"

Pax-o, I assumed, for coffee. I wished I had some. I thought of a former patient of mine, whom I called "Rip van Winkle." Rip would fall asleep even during intercourse. "Let's go on to some more general questions."

"Uh—Eisenhower?"

"No, not him. You told me once that K-PAXians like to contemplate the possibility of traveling forward in time. Remember?"

"Of course."

"Does that mean you can already go backward in time?"

"Not in the sense you mean it. Think—if beings could

146

come back here from, say, EARTH year 2050, why haven't they?"

"Maybe they have."

"I don't see any of them around, do you?"

"So traveling backward in time is impossible?"

"Not at all. But maybe your future beings don't *want* to come back here. Or," he added pointedly, "maybe EARTH's future is limited."

"What about K-PAX? Is it crawling with beings back from the future?"

"Not as far as I know."

"Does that mean—"

"Who knows?"

"All right. You once mentioned a 'spatial fourth dimension.' Have you ever seen it?"

"Once or twice."

"So it exists?"

"Evidently. In fact, while I was back on K-PAX, I managed to stumble into it. It was wonderful—I've always wanted to do that." He paused a moment to ponder the experience. "But I fell out again right away. It must have something to do with gravity."

"Obviously. Okay, let's come down to Earth for a minute."

"Nice place to visit, but . . ."

"Cute. Now—you told me a long time ago that we humans were going 'hell-bent after solar, wind, geothermal, and tidal energy without any thought whatsoever about the consequences.' What did you mean by that?"

"Look. What happens when you dam up a river and steal its energy for your own devices? You flood everything in

147

sight and the river becomes a trickle. So what do you think would happen if you had windmills all over your PLANET?"

"I don't know. What?"

"Use your noggin! For one thing, your climate would be changed to the point where you would think you were on another WORLD. In fact, it's already happening, haven't you noticed? The floods, the droughts, the endless strings of tornadoes and hurricanes—you name it."

"But we don't have all that many windmills on Earth."

"Exactly! And what's going to happen when you have more and more? Not to mention screwing around with your tides and internal temperatures. In the meantime, you insist on burning up the last of your fossil fuels and wreaking havoc as if there were no tomorrow."

"But prot—everything causes *some* pollution or effect on the environment. Until we figure out nuclear fusion, what are we going to use to heat our homes? Run our machines?"

"What, indeed?"

"So there's no way to win?"

"You might try reducing your numbers by five or six billion."

By now I was barely able to keep my eyes open. "But don't you think we're making a beginning? There's a lot of concern these days about the environment, for example."

"*The* environment? You mean *your* environment."

"Well, yes."

"And to make *your* environment more tolerable for *you,* you recycle beer cans, plant trees—is that what you mean?"

"It's a start, isn't it?"

"Recycling is like putting a Band-Aid on a tumor, doc.

And where are you going to plant a tree when there's no place left to plant it?"

"Is that what you meant when you said in your report that we are yet children?"

Prot's gaze shifted to the ceiling, as it often does when he's trying to find words that I might be capable of understanding. I tried unsuccessfully to stifle another yawn.

"Let me put it this way: When you stop making killing seem admirable, when motherhood becomes less important than survival—not just *your* survival, but that of all the other creatures on your PLANET—you'll be on your way to adulthood."

"Lions kill! So do eagles and bears and—"

"They have no choice. You do."

"You kill plants, don't you?"

"Plants have no brain or nervous system. They feel no pain or anguish."

"Is that your main criterion?"

"That is the only criterion."

"What about insects?"

"They have nervous systems, don't they?"

"And you think they feel pain?"

"Have you ever been stepped on?"

"Not literally."

"Try to imagine it."

"Bacteria? Molds?"

"Dig right in."

"Does this mean you're opposed to abortion?"

"I assume you're talking about the *human* fetus."

"Yes."

"If it can feel anxiety or pain, don't do it."

"And does it feel anxiety or pain?"

"It certainly can the day before birth. The day after conception it is no more sensate than a grain of sand."

"Then where do you draw the line?"

"Now, gene, that's a no-brainer, wouldn't you say?"

I had to end this before I fell asleep. "Prot—when are you leaving?"

His eyes rolled up for a moment—his version of a smirk. "I still don't know, daddy-o. But I can tell you this: I filed for three windows this time—just in case."

Suddenly I was wide awake. "Windows?"

"In case things get complicated again."

"With Robert?"

"With everything."

"Can you at least tell me now whether you'll be taking any of our patients with you when you go?"

"*Ad hos forgal!* Not this again!"

"Cassandra?"

He shrugged.

"Jackie?"

"Nah."

"Why not?"

"She's the happiest being in the place!"

"What about—"

"Maybe. She's obviously not happy here. But you have so much to learn from her!"

"From Frankie? A woman who's incapable of love?"

He stared at me disgustedly, almost angrily. "Sometimes I think these visits with you are a complete waste of time. What you call 'love' is a big part of your problem. You tend to limit the concept to yourself and your immediate family.

Talk to frankie, doc. You might learn something. And that goes for all your other patients, too."

I thought: Did Robert's problem have more to do with love than with sex? Was he somehow betrayed by his wife and daughter? Or someone else he loved? "I've got a lot more questions left, my alien friend, but—well, I'll save them for later."

"Fine with me. I've got plenty of other things to do."

"That reminds me. In case I don't get another chance—thanks for what you've done so far. Not only with Robert but for Rudolph and Michael and for getting through to some of the autists. You've accomplished more in the few weeks you've been here than the rest of us have in the past five years."

"I told you before: You can do it, too. All you have to do is eliminate the crap from your thoughts."

"Easy for you to say."

After dinner that evening my wife wouldn't let me work, not even to browse through a journal. Instead, she put on a videotape of *Spellbound*, one of my favorite movies, and suggested I contemplate the possibility of finding a home upstate for our eventual retirement. Within minutes, even before Gregory Peck's first fainting spell, I had fallen asleep.

I dreamed that prot had become fully integrated into Robert, who was no longer shy and depressed, but confident and outgoing. Although he demonstrated no overt traits of prot (he couldn't see ultraviolet light, for example), other signs of him were evident in Robert's personality. His aptitude for math and science increased dramatically and he was making plans to attend college. On the other hand, he had lost none of his (and prot's) sex hangup.

Then the dream took a sudden turn. Prot came flying by accompanied by Manuel. Both of them had sprouted wings. Robert, too, had grown wings and all three of them flew around and around, motioning for me to join in. Then Russell, who looked like an angel out of Revelations, halo and all, lifted off. The other patients appeared, flying in perfect formation, and everyone rose higher and higher, prot in the lead, until they were only a dot against the sun. Desperately I flapped and flapped, but I wasn't able to get off the ground. I tried to call out, but couldn't even do that. In fact, I could hardly breathe. . . .

When I woke up I found Karen watching me with a smile, the one that says, "How sweet." I could tell I had been snoring. The movie was over.

"Decided on a retirement place?"

"No, but it's something I'd definitely like to think about."

I drove in to work the next day, Saturday, but couldn't seem to get much done. I felt listless, out of sorts, not myself. On my desk I uncovered the paper I hadn't yet reviewed, and a couple of tickets I had forgotten about. They were for Carnegie Hall that afternoon. Howie, a fine musician and former patient, had sent them to me. I called Karen, but she had a bowling tournament she wasn't about to miss.

For some reason I thought of prot. He wasn't in the

building, so I tried the lawn. I found him examining the sunflowers, which must have looked like a row of burning stars to him. "Love to hear Howie play!" he exclaimed.

"Hurry up and get ready. We have to leave right away."

"I'm ready," he replied, heading for the gate.

Prot immediately struck up a conversation with the taxi driver, who had seen a picture of him on television. "Glad you're back," he told my alien companion. "I was hopin' you could do somethin' wid dis friggin' heat."

"Sorry, pal," prot replied. "That's up to you." The cabbie didn't say another word.

Later on, we passed a couple of kids banging away at each other with toy rifles. "I see you're still teaching your children to kill," he observed. I thought: I can't take him anywhere!

The multitude in the streets seemed to put him into a foul mood. When I asked him what CD he would take with him if he were marooned on a desert island, he snapped, "Where would I get a cd player on a desert island?"

The concert, however, was a great success. Prot seemed to be able to pick out Howie's playing from the other violinists in the chamber group. "Nice vibrato," he reported. "But he's a hair flat, just like always."

As the musicians started on their final work, the Mendelssohn "Octet," someone in the balcony screamed, "Shut up the goddamn coughing!" The hacking stopped immediately, as did the music. All the players and half the audience gave the man a standing ovation. Prot laughed out loud. Then it became absolutely still. I had never heard the piece played so beautifully.

We visited with Howie after the concert. Looking much younger than he did half a decade earlier, he was very happy to see prot, and wondered how long he'd be around. Prot dodged the question. Howie inquired as to Bess's health, and asked about the patients still with us. "I miss them," he lamented. "In fact, I miss the whole hospital."

"You want to come back?" I joked.

"I'm thinking about it," he replied in all seriousness. "Unless there's room for me on the bus to K-PAX."

Prot didn't say yes, but he didn't say no, either.

SESSION TWENTY-SIX

Villers was late for the Monday-morning staff meeting, explaining that his wife was sick and he had to take her to the doctor. Then there was a delay on the Long Island Rail Road—some "dummkopf" had pulled the emergency cord for no apparent reason.

He was further chagrined by prot's insistence that we turn down the television-appearance fee, but he soon came up with an alternative plan: an appeal for viewer contributions to the hospital, complete with 800 number. The date had been finalized for Wednesday, the twentieth of September. September 20! The day of prot's departure! Unless, of course, he had changed his mind and was waiting for the next "window," whenever that might be. . . .

Goldfarb brought up a new problem, one that hadn't occurred to me. Since my efforts at coaxing Robert out of his protective shell were meeting with some success, was it possible that it might be he, and not prot, who showed up for the taped interview? I said I didn't think that very likely given Robert's reluctance to make an appearance outside my examining room. Beamish pointed out that with prot, no one could be sure of anything. I had no good response to that.

Instead, I discussed the new information that I, or rather prot, had obtained from Bert, but this seemed almost inconsequential compared with Menninger's cheerful report on Charlotte, who had somehow managed to seduce one of the security guards into her cell and nearly bit off his nose and one of his testicles. Our security chief had been apprised of this unfortunate development, of course, and was urged to instruct the guards accordingly.

Villers, still in a foul mood, brought up the scheduled visits by the cetologist and other scientists. He wanted to know how much we were getting for these "consultations" with prot, and was further annoyed with the answer. Thorstein, looking more and more like Klaus's second in command, suggested we charge big bucks for subsequent interviews with Robert's alter ego, particularly if any patents or other useful information were to come of it.

The only other business was a reminder that one of the world's foremost psychotherapists was arriving the next morning for an all-day visit (a brief biography was passed around), and that a popular television personality and author of *Folk Psychology* was coming later in the month.

The conversation then degenerated, as it often does, to discussions of baseball scores, restaurants, weekend retreats, fabulous golf shots, etc. I mused silently about how long prot might be staying. At least until the TV appearance, I assumed, and perhaps longer. And I thought: If the appeal for funds was successful, and he managed to help us raise enough money to finance the new wing, what on Earth would we call it?

After lunch, prot set up an unannounced treasure hunt without saying what the prize might be. That was all the encouragement the patients needed, and they spent the rest of the hour happily combing the lounge, the exercise room, the dining hall, and the quiet room for "buried" treasure. Even though no one knew what he or she was looking for, the joy and excitement were immense.

I was a little annoyed. Prot had not warned me he was going to do this, though technically it wasn't really a "task" for the patients, which he had agreed to tell me about in advance. I watched in both amusement and melancholy as our inmates got into the game with considerable frenzy—everyone searching high and low for something to make their lives more rewarding or, at least, tolerable.

Even some of the staff were caught up in the excitement, turning over chairs and peering under rugs. To tell the truth, I became a participant myself, hoping to find something, I suppose, that would cheer me up, make my day. Perhaps I was searching for the parallel life I had lost, the one in which my father had not died and I had become an opera singer, the one I dream about from time to time.

While all this was going on, however, prot was reported missing. No one had seen him leave. The hunt then became one of finding *him*.

Though further frustrated by this turn of events, I wasn't really worried—it had happened once before. I was sure he would be back in time for our next session. Indeed, it wasn't long after his disappearance that Giselle came running in, shouting that he had shown up again, to loud cheers from his followers. Whatever he had done while he was away had taken him no time at all, apparently.

My dream didn't come true that day, and I doubt that anyone else's did either. But each of the patients turned up his very own gossamer thread, invisible to everyone else. Something to give them hope for a better world, perhaps, a tenuous new lease on life.

I wondered whether my frustration showed when prot came in, followed by a cat. He sat down and started on a plum, which he shared with his "friend." I didn't even know cats liked fruit.

"Where's Robert?"

"He'll be along shortly. He's still pumping himself up. Besides," he added wistfully, "I hardly ever get any fruit anymore."

"You want to tell me where you went this afternoon?"

"Not really."

"You promised to let me know if you were planning any trips, remember?"

"I didn't plan it. It was a spur-of-the-moment thing."

"Where did you go?"

"I had some invitations to deliver."

"Personally?"

"I'm not a 'person,' remember? I'm a being."

"Why didn't you just drop them in the mailbox?"

"I wanted to be sure they got there."

"To people who are going to K-PAX with you?"

"Some are people, some aren't."

"So how many invitations were there?"

I didn't expect an answer to that one either, but he replied, cheerfully, "Only a dozen so far. Still plenty of room."

I glared at him. "Next time you plan any 'spur-of-the-moment things,' will you let me know, please?"

"It's your party."

"Thank you. Now—what about Robert?"

"What about hi—"

"Dammit, prot, did he tell you what happened to him when he was five?"

"Yes, and may I say: You human beings are sick!"

"Not everyone, prot. Just some of us."

"From what I've seen, you're all capable of just about anything."

We sat staring at each other for a while. Five or six plums later, he spat the last pit into the bowl and placed his hands behind his head, apparently sated. The cat lounged contentedly in his lap. Prot's eyes drooped shut. Suddenly he leaned forward and wrapped his arms around himself. Robert's eyes fought to reopen. He seemed weak, shaken, his confidence gone. In short, he looked much as he had in earlier sessions. Instinctively, he began stroking the cat, which purred noisily.

"Hello, Rob, it's good to see you again. How are you feeling today?"

"I'm afraid."

"Please trust me. No harm will come to you in this

room. This is your safe haven, remember? We're just going to chat about whatever you'd like to tell me. Whatever comes into your mind. We'll proceed at your own pace."

"All right. But I'm still scared."

"I understand."

He sat looking at me, but said nothing for several precious minutes.

I took a chance. "Is there anything you want to tell me about the time your father was in the hospital?"

His gaze dropped to the floor. "Yes."

I was elated. Thanks to prot, Robert had made such excellent progress that hypnosis might not be necessary.

"You went to live with your Uncle Dave and Aunt Catherine, is that right?"

"Yes," he murmured.

"Are they on your father's or mother's side of the family?"

Rob slowly looked up. "Uncle Dave was Mom's brother."

"And Aunt Catherine was his wife?"

"No. His sister. Mom's sister."

"And they lived together?"

"Neither of them ever married."

"All right. Can you tell me a little about them?"

"They were both big. Heavyset. My mother's a little plump, too."

"What else? What were they like?"

"They were not very nice people."

"In what way?"

"They were mean. Cruel. But nobody knew that when I went to live with them."

"What sorts of mean things did they do?"

160

"Uncle Dave killed my kitten." He unconsciously picked up the cat and hugged it.

"He did? Why?"

"He wanted to teach me a lesson."

"What lesson?"

Robert turned noticeably paler. His face became contorted by uncontrollable tics. "I . . . I don't remember."

"Try, Rob. I think you're ready to talk about this now. What did your uncle do to you? Will you tell me?"

There was a long pause. I had just about decided to hypnotize him when he said, so weakly that I could barely hear him, "I had to sleep on the living-room sofa. The first night I was there he came downstairs and woke me up."

"Why did he wake you up?"

"He wanted to lie down with me."

"And did he do that?"

"Yes. I didn't want him to. There wasn't room on the sofa for him and me both. But he got in with me anyway."

"What happened then?"

"He put his hand in my pajamas. I kept saying, 'No!' But he wouldn't listen. I was crushed against the back of the sofa and couldn't move."

"What did he do?"

"He licked my face with his big tongue. Then he felt me for a long time until—"

"Until what, Rob?"

"Until it started to get bigger."

"What did you think about that?"

"I was afraid. I didn't understand what was happening. I didn't know what to do."

"What happened then?"

"He finally got up and left."

"Just like that?"

"He said if I told anyone he would kill my kitten."

"What else?"

"The outside of my pajamas was sticky and cold. I didn't know why."

"Where did he go?"

"He went back upstairs."

"Did this ever happen again?"

"Almost every night. I used to lie there and pray that Uncle Dave wouldn't come down."

"Was it always the same?"

"No. Sometimes he put his mouth down there. Then— Then he—"

"I know this is difficult, Rob. But you must try to tell me the rest."

"He wanted me to put my mouth on him! Oh, Daddy, help!"

"And did you do it?"

"No! I said, 'No—I won't do it!' "

"And he left you alone after that?"

"No. The next day he killed my kitten. He picked her up and wrung her neck."

"While you watched?"

"Yes."

"What else?"

"He said he was going to do that to me unless I did what he wanted."

"Did he come back that night?"

"Yes."

"And did you do it?"

"No. I don't know. I . . . I . . . I don't remember anymore."

"What's the next thing you remember?"

"He came back about every night but I don't think he bothered me. I was always asleep."

"You were able to fall asleep knowing your uncle was coming to molest you?"

"Not exactly. I never fell asleep until he came down and got into the sofa. So I don't think he did much after that."

"Where was your Aunt Catherine all those nights?"

"She stayed upstairs, mostly. She had a bad heart. But sometimes I thought I saw her sitting on the stairs. And I heard her once or twice."

"What did she say?"

"Nothing. She just made funny noises. Like she couldn't breathe."

"And this went on until your father came home from the hospital?"

"Yes. They killed a dog, too."

"What dog?"

"I don't know. I think it was a stray. They killed it with a knife."

"Why?"

"They said that would happen to me if I told. Uncle Dave would strangle me and Aunt Catherine would stab me with the knife."

"Did you ever tell anyone?"

"Never."

"All right, Rob. We'll stop for a while."

Obviously relieved, he sighed loudly.

"Thank you for telling me all this. Are you okay?"

"I don't know. I think so." He began stroking the cat again.

I let him rest for a minute. I should have sent him back to the wards at this point, but I knew prot could depart at any time despite everything. "Rob, I'd like to put you under hypnosis now. Would that be all right?"

His shoulders slumped even lower. "I thought we were finished for today."

"Almost."

He looked left and then right, as if trying to find a way out. "All right. If you think it will help. . . ."

As before, he didn't go into the trance immediately, as prot always did, but more cautiously, fighting all the way. When I was sure he was "asleep" I induced him to return to the past, but this time all the way back to his fifth birthday. He described the cake, remembered blowing out all the candles. But he wouldn't tell me his wish or (he solemnly informed me) it wouldn't come true. It was only a short time later that his father was injured in the slaughterhouse and ended up in the hospital, and little Robin (his boyhood name) had to go live with his Uncle Dave and Aunt Catherine for a few weeks. The prospect was not an unpleasant one for him. He seemed to like his mother's older siblings, who had given him a kitten for his birthday. His sisters were taken to live with another aunt in Billings.

"All right, Robin, you're at your aunt and uncle's house and it's time for bed. Where are you going to sleep?"

"Aunt Catherine made the sofa into a bed for me. I like it. It smells funny, but it's soft and warm."

"Good. Are you going to sleep now?"

"Yes."

"Where is the kitten?"

"Uncle Dave put her in the kitchen."

"All right. What's happening now?"

"I'm just laying here, listening to the crickets. The kitten is meowing. Oh—someone's here. It's Uncle Dave. He's trying to get in bed with me. He is pushing me over."

"He's coming to sleep with you?"

"I guess so. But it's too crowded. He's pushing me against the back of the sofa. He has his arm around me. He's touching me! 'No, Uncle Dave! I don't want you to!' He's putting his hand in my pajamas. He's feeling my thing. 'Uncle Dave! Please don't. I'll tell!' "

"What did he say to that?"

Five-year-old Robert started to cry. "He says if I do he'll kill my kitten."

"It's all right, Robin. He's finished now. He's gone back upstairs. Just rest for a little while."

He continued to sob until it tapered off to a whimper.

"All right, Robin, now it's one week later, and you're getting into the sofa. How are you feeling?"

"I'm very afraid. He's going to come down. I know he's going to come down. I can't sleep. I'm so scared."

"Where is your kitten?"

"Oh, he killed her. He killed her. I think he's going to kill me, too." He was shaking. "Oh, here he comes. 'Please, Uncle Dave, please. Please God, don't do it tonight!' "

"He's getting into the sofa?"

"No. He's pulling my blanket off. I'm holding on to it but he's too strong. Now he's taking off his pajamas. I don't want to look. I'm going to sleep now." He closed his eyes tightly.

"Robin? Are you asleep? Robin?"

His eyes came open again. But the look of fear was gone, replaced by one of hatred. Bitter, intense hatred. All his muscles were tense. He said nothing.

"Rob?"

"No," he replied, through clenched teeth.

"Who are you?"

His feet began to shuffle. "Harry."

I was stunned. Not because another alter had made an appearance, but because I understood immediately what a fool I'd been, that there might be still others I didn't yet know about, perhaps watching and listening to everything that transpired. "Harry, please—tell me what's happening."

The feet stopped shuffling. "He's kneeling beside the sofa. His thing is in my face. He wants me to put it in my mouth."

"Are you doing that?"

"I have to or he will kill Robin. But I will kill *him*, too. If he does anything to Robin I will kill him. I hate him! I hate his guts! I hate his rotten thing! I am going to bite it off if he hurts Robin. Then I will kill him. I will! I will! And her, too, that fat pig." He looked as though he meant every word.

"All right, Harry. It's all over now. Uncle Dave and Aunt Catherine have gone upstairs. You are all alone. You and Robin."

Harry sat in his chair spitting violently, glowering, his eyes rising as the pair made their way slowly up the stairs.

"Harry? Listen carefully. You're going to sleep now." I waited until he calmed down, closed his eyes. A moment later I whispered, "All right, Robin. It's morning now. Robin, wake up."

"Huh?"

"Is that you, Robin?"

"Yes."

"It's time to get up."

Dismally: "I don't want to get up." But at least the horrible twitching had subsided.

"I understand. It's okay. Just rest there for a while. We're going to go forward in time now. You're getting older. You're six, now you're seven, now ten. Now you're fifteen, twenty, twenty-five, thirty, thirty-five, thirty-eight. Rob?"

"Yes?"

"How are you doing?"

"Not so hot."

"All right, I'm going to wake you up now. I'm going to count backward from five. By the time I get to one you will be wide awake and feeling fine. Five . . . four . . . three . . . two . . . one." I snapped my fingers. "Hello, Rob—how do you feel?"

I needn't have asked. He may have felt fine, but he looked sick and exhausted. "Can I go to my room now?"

"Of course. And Rob?"

"Yes?"

I got up, placed my hand on his shoulder, and escorted him to the door. He was still holding the cat. "I think the worst is over. Everything is going to be all right now."

"Do you really think so?"

"Yes, I do. In one or two more sessions I think we'll have everything sorted out. Then you can begin to get well."

"That sounds too wonderful to be true."

"It's true. And when you get better, it will be perfectly all right for prot to leave. You won't need him anymore."

"I hope not. I don't think he's going to be around much longer anyway, no matter what happens."

"Do you have any idea—"

"You're browbeating again, coach. He doesn't know, and neither do I."

"Prot! Rob was just on his way back to Ward Two."

He shrugged and reached for the door.

"Before you go, tell me: Are there any child molesters on K-PAX?"

"No, and no adult molesters, either."

On Tuesday morning one of the world's foremost psychiatrists arrived to spend the day at MPI meeting with faculty and staff, and to present a seminar on current research in his field. I had never met the man before, though I had read most of his books, including the immensely popular *The Lighter Side of Mental Illness*, heard him lecture at national and international conferences, and was looking forward to this rare opportunity.

He strode into the hospital wearing top hat and tails, his trademark dress. Now in his eighties, he looks twenty years younger, and keeps himself in shape by running seven miles every morning before breakfast, doing fifty push-ups at midday, and swimming an hour every afternoon before dinner. In between he gulps vitamins and minerals by the handful. He asked everyone he met where the swimming pool was. Unfortunately, the Manhattan Psychiatric Institute does not have such a facility.

I didn't see him until later, in part because I skipped the morning coffee conference (our guest had grapefruit juice) in order to visit Russell, who was in the infirmary, apparently suffering from exhaustion. He seemed okay otherwise, and was still preaching the imminent demise of the world.

I spoke to Chak about Russ's condition, but he was mystified about what was ailing him. "You are not to worry," he assured me. "He is not in immediate danger." He was thinking of transferring him to Columbia Presbyterian for further examination and testing.

"Do what you need to do," I said. "I would hate to lose him."

I poked my head into Russell's room before leaving the clinic to wave a cheerful good-bye and found him weeping. I stepped in and asked him what the matter was. He said, "When I get to heaven I hope they have hamburgers on Saturday nights. . . ." I think it was the first time I had ever heard him say anything that wasn't a quote from the Bible.

My turn to speak privately with the great clinician, whose books occupy a prominent place on my office shelves, came at two o'clock. He bounded into my office fresh as a kid (thanks to the push-ups, perhaps), swallowed several vitamin pills, and immediately fell asleep sitting up in his chair. For a moment I thought he had died there, but on careful observation I could see his chest moving under his cravat. Not wanting to disturb him, I slipped out and let him have his forty winks. It was only later that I learned he had passed out in everyone's office. Apparently he was saving his strength for the four-o'clock seminar.

When I returned to awaken and escort him to Beamish's office he finished the sentence he had started when he dozed off and leaped out of the chair like a twenty-year-old. I had a difficult time keeping up with him as he winged his way down the corridor.

Having an hour or so free before the seminar, I decided to spend them on the grounds, where I found Lou huffing and puffing around the back forty. Not having seen him for a couple of weeks I was aghast at the amount of weight he had put on. His maternity slacks were stretched to their limit. His bright-yellow blouse was unbuttoned and it fell over his swollen belly like the petals of a giant sunflower. It appeared he was literally feeding his delusion.

He blew some hair from his eyes. "Had I known it was going to be like this I never would have become a mother," he groaned. He seemed to be fingering something—a gossamer thread, I supposed.

I noticed Dustin plodding along the far wall. He always seemed to be most agitated late in the afternoon. I heard Lou say, "Why don't you give Dustin a break and keep his parents away from him tonight?"

"They're nice people, Lou. And they're his only visitors."

"They're driving him nuts!"

Just then Milton wiggled along on his beat-up unicycle, juggling a few raisins and mumbling to himself, "And I told the maestro, 'No, thank you! I want to hear the entire *ramide* or no *ramide* at all!'"

Virginia Goldfarb came by from the other direction and reminded me of the upcoming seminar by our distinguished visitor. I accompanied her to the amphitheater.

When everyone was seated and Villers had introduced our guest in a very complimentary fashion, he bounded from his chair and took the podium. It looked to be a rewarding hour. Unfortunately, when the lights were dimmed for his slides, the great man fell asleep again, and he stood snoring softly at the front of the room like an old horse wearing a top hat. The projectionist, one of our bright young residents, gravely continued with the slide show, which was pretty much self-explanatory anyway. When it was over and the lights came up, our speaker awakened, concluded his talk, and asked for questions.

No one had any. Perhaps everyone else was thinking, as I was, about the functional capacities of the elderly gentlemen who populate the halls of Congress and the United States Supreme Court, sleeping at the switch, so to speak, while the trains roll by.

Refreshed by his nap, our distinguished colleague got in his hour of swimming at a local gym before taking another snooze, this time over dinner at one of Manhattan's finest restaurants. (Villers, whose wife was still sick, had begged off and I was left to deal with the problem myself.) Somehow he managed to catch his menu on fire from the candle and, later, his head fell into his plate and mashed his "very young, tender sweet peas in unsalted butter sauce with a hush of marjoram and dill." After helping him eat, I finally got our slumbering guest into a cab and off to the airport, his forehead still flecked with food. He strode briskly into the terminal, but whether he made it home or not is anybody's guess.

As we pulled away I marveled at the accomplishments

of our illustrious friend, much of which must have taken place while he was sound asleep. And I wondered whether he might not have a good deal more energy if he didn't keep himself in such great shape.

SESSION TWENTY-SEVEN

Early Wednesday afternoon, before my next session with Robert, I had a quick lunch with Giselle just to touch base. She mentioned that an ophthalmologist she knew was extremely interested in proving or disproving prot's ability to see UV light. I asked that she put him off for the moment. "Prot may be leaving soon, and there's still a lot of work to do."

"That's exactly why he should see prot ASAP!"

I told her I would let her know when a good opportunity came up.

Unfortunately, she was unable to tell me anything about prot I didn't already know. In fact, she complained that he was spending less time with her than he had earlier, and she requested copies of the taped recordings of our last few sessions. I felt sorry for her—she had become like a daughter to me—but I refused to let her listen to the tapes.

"Why not?" she demanded. "It's going into your book, isn't it? Then the whole world will know everything he said in those sessions."

"Not everything. Besides—what makes you so sure I'm going to write another book?"

"Because you want to retire. At least your wife wants you to."

"A book isn't going to do it."

"It'll help."

"Maybe, but I still can't tell you. You know about doctor-patient privilege. If I do the book I won't identify any of the patients by their real names."

Her cheek ballooned with half a sandwich. "So don't tell me who's on the tapes!"

"Why not ask prot to tell you about the sessions? He seems to have a pretty good memory."

"I tried that."

"What did he say?"

"He doesn't want to violate your privacy."

"What does *that* mean?"

"I think he knows all there is to know about you."

"There isn't that much to know," I said, uncomfortably.

"He says we all have a lot of secrets we don't want any other being to find out about."

"Well, he's probably right about that."

"Yes, and everything else, too. In fact, it was prot's idea that I listen to the tapes. He says I can help Robert more if I know what's going on."

The retirement bug buzzed in my ear. "I'll think about it," I told her.

Robert strode in for his twenty-seventh session with an uncharacteristic smile on his face. Not a prot-like smirk, but certainly a grin. For the first time he actually appeared eager to talk. He hadn't even brought a cat with him.

"Rob, are you ready to tell me about Sally and Rebecca?"

The smile shrank but he said, "Yes, I think I am."

"Good. We'll stop if you begin to feel uncomfortable."

He nodded.

"Rob, how can you be sure you're not Rebecca's father?"

"Sally and I never had sex—uh—sexual intercourse."

"What did you have?"

"We just kissed and petted. That was all we did."

"Even after you were married?"

"Yes."

"Did you ever find yourself with your clothes off?"

"Sometimes."

"How did you think that happened?"

"They came off while we were kissing and petting."

"But nothing else happened?"

"No." Robert suddenly seemed less confident. He stared at his feet.

"How are you doing?"

"I'm okay."

"Do you know what sex is? How it operates?"

Uncomfortably: "I have a vague idea."

"But you've never done it."

"No."

"Sally wasn't interested?"

"Oh, yes. She was."

"Didn't you want to make love with her?"

"Yes. No. I don't know. We never—"

"All right. Let's not waste any more time. If you're ready, I'd like to hypnotize you again."

He looked away.

"Rob, this will probably be the last time. We're very close to the heart of your difficulty. Do you trust me?"

He took a deep breath and exhaled it harshly. "Yes."

"Good. Are you ready now?"

He took another breath and nodded. Slowly, kicking and scratching all the way, he fell into a trance. I took him back to June 9, 1975. "Rob, you and Sally have just been married. Do you remember that moment?"

"Of course. Our families were all there and it was a beautiful service."

"And after that?"

"There was a reception in the church basement. Cake and punch and some cashews and blue candy in little silver dishes."

"Okay. The reception is over. What is happening now?"

"People are snapping our pictures."

"And after that?"

"We're leaving the church. Everyone is throwing rice at us as we run down the steps and out to the car."

"You bought a car?"

"Yes. A '57 Ford Fairlane."

"Where did you get the money?"

"We used our wedding money for the down payment."

"Go on."

"We're driving away."

"Where are you going?"

"We don't have enough money for a honeymoon, so we're just going for a drive out in the country. It's a beautiful spring day. It's wonderful having Sally next to me with her head on my shoulder."

"I'm sure it is. All right, it's early evening. Where are you now?"

"The Hilltop House."

"What's the Hilltop House?"

"It's a nice restaurant in Maroney. About fifty miles from Guelph."

"How is the dinner?"

"Terrific. The best one we've ever had."

"What are you eating?"

"Lobster. We've never had it before."

"Okay. Dinner is over. Where are you going now?"

"We're driving home."

"Where is home?"

"Back in Guelph. A trailer park called Restful Haven."

"You have a trailer?"

"Sally prefers to call it a mobile home."

"Do you own it or rent it?"

"It was a present from Sally's family. It's a used one."

"All right. You're home now. What's happening?"

"We're going inside. I forgot to carry Sally over the threshold, so we're going back out and I'm picking her up and carrying her in. She's kissing me."

"What do you see, now that you're inside?"

"Somebody has put a box of diapers on the kitchen table. For a joke, I guess."

"Is Sally pregnant?"

"Yes."

"Who knows about this?"

"Probably everyone."

"You mean word gets around."

"Yes."

"Does the father know?"

"I don't know who the father is. Maybe Sally told him. We never talked about it."

"What's happening now?"

"It's starting to get dark. I'm not tired, but Sally wants to go to bed."

"Is she doing that?"

"Yes. She's in our little bathroom . . . now she's coming out. She's wearing a silk nightie. While she was in there I took off my clothes and got into bed."

"And is Sally getting in with you?"

"Yes. Actually she's jumping up and down on the bed and laughing."

"How do you feel about that?"

"I'm afraid."

"What are you afraid of?"

"We have never had sex. I've never done it with anyone. Except—"

"Yes, I know about Uncle Dave."

No response.

"All right. What is happening now?"

"Sally is snuggling up to me, rubbing her hand on my bare chest. She's kissing my face and my neck. All of a sudden I'm very sleepy. I'm falling asleep."

"Rob? Are you asleep?"

"Are you kidding? At a time like this?" His demeanor

suddenly changed. He was alert, almost bug-eyed. He seemed quite agitated. But it wasn't prot. Or Harry.

"Who are you?"

"Never fear, Paul is here."

"Paul? You're Paul? What are you doing here?"

"Helping out."

"How are you helping out?"

"Sally is horny as hell. She needs me. So does Rob."

"Rob? How does Rob need you?"

"I'm showing Rob how to make love to his wife."

"But he's asleep."

"Yeah, he always does that. But that's not my problem." He turned over and began to make kissing sounds.

"All right, Paul. It's an hour later. It's all over. Sally's asleep. What are you doing now?"

"Just lying here. Sally's head is on my shoulder. She is sound asleep. I can hear her breathing. I can smell her breath. Is that what lobster smells like?"

"Aren't you sleepy?"

"A little. I'm just going to lie here and enjoy this until I doze off." He was smiling.

"How many times has this happened before?"

"Not too many. Until now. It's been hard to find any privacy anywhere."

"Paul, are you the father of Sally's child?"

He started snapping his fingers. "How'd you guess?"

"It wasn't too difficult. Tell me: Can you hear everything that goes on with Rob?"

"Sure."

"Does he know about you?"

Snap, snap, snap. "Nope."

"How often do you come out?"

"Only when Sally needs me."

"Why not any other time?"

"Why should I? I've got a pretty good deal, don't you think?"

"From your point of view, I suppose it is. Okay, just one or two more questions."

"Shoot." *Snappity snap snap.*

"When did you first make an appearance?"

"Oh, I guess Rob was eleven or twelve."

"And he needed to masturbate?"

"He'd freak out every time he got a hard-on."

"All right. One last thing: Do you know about Harry?"

"Sure. Nasty little kid."

"All right. You lie there a while. It's getting late. You are falling asleep." Still smiling, he closed his eyes and the finger-snapping stopped. "Now it's morning. Time to get up."

His eyes opened, but he was no longer smiling.

"Rob? Is that you?"

He yawned. "Yes. What time is it?"

"It's still early. Is Sally there with you?"

"Shh. She's sleeping. God, she's beautiful."

I lowered my voice. "I'm sure she is. Now we're going to come forward in time. Imagine a calendar whose pages are turning rapidly forward. It's 1975, 1980, 1985, 1990, 1995. We're back in the present—September 13, 1995. Do you understand?"

"I understand."

I woke him up. He looked tired, but not nearly so exhausted as he had been after the previous session. "Rob, do you remember anything that just happened?"

"You were going to hypnotize me."

"Yes."

"Did you?"

"Uh-huh. And I think we've got most of the puzzle put together now."

"I'm glad to hear that." He seemed greatly relieved, though he didn't yet know what the picture looked like.

"I'm going to tell you something now that you might find very disturbing. Please remember at all times that I'm trying to help you deal with your very understandable grief and confusion."

"I know."

"And remember that you can do or say anything that comes to mind. You are in your safe haven here."

"I remember."

"Good. Most of what we've learned about your past has come about through hypnosis. That's because when a person is hypnotized he is able to recall many things that his conscious mind has repressed. Do you understand?"

"I think so."

"Okay. I've hypnotized you several times now, and each time you told me some things about your past that you have consciously forgotten. Primarily because they are too painful to remember."

Robert seemed to freeze for a moment and, just as suddenly, thawed. It became clear to me then, if it wasn't before, how much he wanted to get well. I felt enormously gratified. "At some point I'm going to let you hear the tapes of all the sessions we've had so far. For now I'm just going to summarize everything we've learned to this point. If it gets too rough, just stop me and we'll pick it up some other time."

"I trust you. Please tell me what happened, for God's sake."

I told him the whole story, beginning with his burning his hand on the stove, the lumbering cow, about his father's accident and hospitalization, and about Uncle Dave and Aunt Catherine. He listened with the most rapt attention until Uncle Dave came down the stairs. At that point he shouted "No!" and buried his face in his hands. A moment later he lifted his head. I was sure it would be prot, or maybe someone else. But it was still Rob. As they used to say in the movies, he had "passed the crisis."

He asked me to go on. I told him about Harry. He shook his head as if he didn't believe it, but then he nodded for me to continue. I brought up the subject of his father's death and the first few appearances of prot, on up to his junior year of high school and his first date with Sally, her pregnancy, their wedding, and Paul. Again he wagged his head, but this time he merely stared off into space as if testing the logic behind it all. "Paul, you rotten son of a bitch," he blurted out, before breaking into a single, loud sob. That was what I had been waiting to hear.

"Paul is the father of your child."

"I figured as much."

"Do you understand what I'm telling you?"

"What do you mean?"

"The fact is that *you* were Rebecca's father. Paul is you. So is Harry. And so, believe it or not, is prot."

"That's pretty hard to swallow."

"I think you're ready to try. I'm going to make a copy of all the tapes and I want you to listen to them. Will you do that?"

182

"Yes."

"Good. It would be best if you did it here and left prot outside. I don't have any patient interviews Friday morning. I can ask Betty to bring you up then. Will you come and listen to the first three or four? If that works out you can hear the rest later on."

"I'll try."

"I'm also going to give you some reading material. A few case histories of multiple personality disorder."

"I'll read them, I promise. I'll do anything you say."

"Good."

"Only—"

"Only what?"

"Only—what happens next?"

"There are still a couple of loose ends to tie up. We'll try to do that next session. Then the real work begins."

"What kind of work?"

"It's called integration. We need to bring you and prot and Paul and Harry into one single personality. That won't be easy. It will depend a great deal on how badly you want to get well."

"I'll do my best, Dr. Brewer. But . . ."

"Yes?"

"What will happen to them? Will they just disappear?"

"No. They'll always be with you. They'll always be a part of you."

"I don't think prot's going to like that."

"Why don't you ask him?"

"I will. Right now he's hibernating again."

"All right. I want you to go back to your room and think about everything we've talked about."

He turned to go. Then he stopped and said, "Dr. Brewer?"

"Yes?"

"I have never been so happy in my life. And I don't even know why."

"We'll try to find out together, Rob. One last thing. Except for my home in Connecticut you have been able to talk to me only in this room. From now on I want you to consider all of Ward Two your safe haven. Will you do that?"

"I'll sure as hell try."

Our time had run over. I was late for an executive committee meeting and I couldn't have cared less.

It wasn't quite that easy, of course—it was prot who returned to the wards. But I got a call from Betty that evening. She, in turn, had been phoned by one of the night nurses. Robert had made his first appearance in Ward Two. It happened in the lounge while he was watching a chess match. He kibitzed! It definitely wasn't prot, who took no part in such "trivia." He didn't stay out long—he was just testing the waters—but it was a glorious beginning.

Just before the scheduled trip to the zoo I made it a point to seek out prot, for two reasons. First, I wanted to make certain that it was he, and not Robert, who was going. And second, I wanted to ask him about Russell, who seemed to be languishing in the hospital, though the doctors couldn't find much wrong with him.

I found him on the lawn surrounded by his usual coterie of patients and cats. As always, there was a certain amount of grumbling when I asked them all to excuse us, though everyone was eagerly awaiting the visit to the zoo and seemed to be in good spirits. He winked at them, promising he would rejoin them in a few minutes. "What's wrong with Russell?" I asked him when we were alone.

"Nothing."

"Nothing? He won't eat. He won't even get out of bed."

"That often happens when a being is preparing to die."

"Die? You just said nothing is wrong with him."

"That's right. Every being dies. Perfectly normal procedure."

"You mean he *wants* to die?"

"He's ready to leave EARTH. He wants to go home."

"Uh—you mean heaven?"

"Yep."

I spotted Jackie somersaulting on the lawn. She, too, was happily anticipating an adventure. "But you don't believe in heaven, do you, prot?"

"No, but *he* does. And with human beings, believing is the same as truth, isn't it?"

"Can you help him?"

"Help him die?"

"No, dammit, help him live!"

"If he wants to die, that's his right, don't you think? Besides, he'll be back."

I thought for a moment he was talking about the second coming. Then I remembered his theory about the collapse of the universe and the reversal of time. I threw up my hands and walked off. How do you reason with a crazy person?

As I was trudging back into the building I met Giselle and some of the nurses and security guards coming out. They all grinned and waved, delighted, like the patients, to be having a rare outing, away from all this. I wouldn't have minded the trip myself, despite the heat and humidity, but I had to attend some meetings for Villers, whose wife was having surgery in the same hospital where Russell was calmly awaiting the end.

Rudolph and Michael were both discharged that morning, and I was more than elated to sign the release papers and escort them to the gate. Not as happy as they were, though. Particularly Mike, who was to take an EMS orientation class the following week. Rudolph, a totally different person from his former self, shook hands and wished me good luck with the rest of the patients. "But don't let prot get away," he admonished. "He's the best doctor you have."

That same evening, after everyone had returned from the zoo, Rob asked Dustin (who was perfectly normal at the chessboard) for a game. Rob lost that battle, and the next several as well, but he appeared, at last, to be winning the war.

I got another report that Villers had spent a rare night at MPI, sitting up until dawn talking with Cassandra. He was unshaven and not wearing a tie, something I myself had never seen. I couldn't believe he was only looking for racing tips, and I wondered whether his wife's illness might not be more serious than he let on. I made a mental note to ask him about it as soon as I found time.

SESSION TWENTY-EIGHT

The Bronx Zoo is one of the premier animal-holding facilities in the United States. Occupying more than 250 acres in the heart of a major metropolitan area, it is the biggest urban sanctuary in the world. Noted for its attempts to preserve many of the planet's endangered species, it houses such diverse specimens as Père David's deer and the European bison, not to mention a variety of rare rodents, snakes, and insects.

The original idea had been to take only those patients from One and Two who were deemed capable of handling the trip. Prot vetoed this, pointing out that permanent harm could come to those who wanted to come but were not permitted. Thus, about thirty-five of our inmates boarded the bus that morning, all those (except for the residents of Ward Four) who had expressed a desire to go. They were divided into groups of six, each accompanied by three staff members—a clinical trainee, a nurse, an orderly or security guard—and a zoo volunteer.

Giselle reported to me the following morning that the outing was a tremendous success for everyone concerned, greatly boosting morale for the staff as well as the patients, and plans were soon in the works for a series of four trips a year: the zoo, the Museum of Natural History, Central Park, and the Metropolitan Museum of Art.

Prot's reaction varied from ecstasy at seeing so many different animals, to depression in finding all of them "incarcerated without benefit of trial." He proceeded from cage to cage, compound to compound, stopping at each to visit the inhabitants, and wherever he went, the elephants or zebras or swans ran trumpeting and honking to congregate as close to him as possible. He, in turn, seemed to "reassure" them, uttering various peculiar sounds and making subtle gestures. According to Giselle, the animals seemed, for all the world, to be listening to what he had to say, and he to them.

But the loudest supplicants were the chimpanzees and gorillas, who whined and screeched like so many pleading children. Prot, in turn, caused further commotion among the security people and zoo volunteers by leaping over the retaining wall and poking his fingers through the wire screens for a touch, which immediately quieted the apes, if not his hosts.

Whether any information was conveyed by this means is not certain, but we have had reports from zoo officials that many of their charges have changed their behavior patterns significantly following prot's visit. For example, the bears and tigers have ceased their endless pacing, and the incidence of bizarre conduct and self-mutilation among the primates has decreased substantially. When Giselle asked him what the animals were "telling" him, he replied, "They're saying: 'Help! Let us out!'" And how did he respond to that? "I encouraged them all to hang in there— the way things are going, the humans won't be around much longer."

Of course none of this proves that anything was communicated between prot and the zoo's inhabitants. In order to test this possibility, Giselle asked him to write down any information he had obtained from them (e.g., their personal histories, which neither she nor prot would have had in their possession). When she gets his account, she plans to meet with zoo officials to determine whether there is anything of value in all this.

The only negative aspect of the outing was that some of the other patients managed to reach a conclusion similar to that of prot's, demanding to know why the zoo's inhabitants had been locked up, what crimes they had committed. Perhaps this concern had less to do with the animals themselves than with their own virtual imprisonment, which, in many cases, they see as unwarranted. Prot, for his part, has often reminded me that it's the people outside the mental institutions who should be in here, and vice versa.

I still don't know whether prot can talk to animals, but all that pales in comparison to what happened later that morning. As usual, I missed the whole thing, but those who saw it made sure I was filled in.

I was looking for Lou to see if he was still gaining weight when a contingent of manics, delusionals, and compulsives came running toward me, raving and shouting. I was beginning to feel some trepidation—were they upset that prot was disappearing on occasion and leaving Robert behind?—when one of them yelled that it was time to send Manuel home.

"Why?" I asked.

"Because he just flew across the lawn!"

"Where is he?"

"He's still out there!"

A cadre of patients trailing behind me, I headed down the stairs and out the front door, where I found Manuel sitting on the steps, his head in his hands. He was unashamedly crying.

"I've wanted to do that for so long . . ." he sobbed. "Now I can die."

"Do you want to die, Manny?"

"No, no, no, it's not that. It's just that I was so afraid I would die before I flew, and my life would be for nothing. Now that I can die, it's all right to live. I'm not afraid anymore."

That made some sense, I suppose, at least to Manuel. "How did you do it, Manny? How did you get off the ground?"

"I don't know," he confessed, with just a hint of Hispanic accent. "Prot said I needed to imagine exactly what it would be like to fly, down to the last tiny detail. I tried so much. I concentrated so hard. . . ." He closed his dark, shining eyes and his head tilted left, then right, as if he were reliving his imagined flight. "All of a sudden I knew how to do it!"

"I'm going to ask Dr. Thorstein to meet with you as soon as he can, all right? I think you'll be moving down to Ward One before long."

Sniffling quietly, he said, matter-of-factly, "Everything is okay now."

By this time some of the staff were also gathered around him. I asked one of the nurses whether any of them had seen Manuel lift off. No one had. Only the patients had witnessed this incredible feat.

Did they all lie? Not likely. Did Manuel fly? Also unlikely, though they claim he soared like an eagle. The important thing is that *he* believes it. From that day on he never flapped his arms again. His lifelong dream accomplished, he was happy, self-confident, at peace with the world.

I forgot all about Lou.

As soon as he came into my examining room I asked Rob whether he had read all the material I had given him, and listened to the tapes.

"Oh, yes," he said. "It's hard to believe, but I think everything you told me is true." I gazed into his eyes for signs of uncertainty or even duplicity, and found none. Nor did he look away.

"I do, too. And I think we have nearly the whole story. There's just one missing piece of the puzzle. Will you help me fit it in?"

"I'll try."

"It has to do with your wife and daughter."

He sighed loudly. "I wondered when you were going to get to that."

"It's time, Rob. And I think you can handle it now."

"I'm not so sure of that, but I want to try."

"Good. I think we can do this without hypnosis. I just want you to tell me whatever you can about the day you came home from the slaughterhouse and found a man coming out your front door."

Rob stared straight ahead and said nothing.

"You chased him back into the house," I prodded, "through the kitchen and out the rear door. The sprinkler was still going. Do you remember any of that?"

Tears welled up in his eyes.

"Do you remember what happened next, Rob? This is very important."

"I caught up with the man and wrestled him to the ground."

"What happened then?"

The tears were rolling down his face. But I could tell he was thinking hard, trying to remember what he had done to the intruder who had killed his wife and daughter. His eyes darted back and forth along the wall, to my chair, to the ceiling. Finally, he said, "I don't really know. The next thing I remember is coming into the house and carrying Sally and Becky to their beds."

"And then you mopped the kitchen, said your good-byes, and headed for the river."

"I wanted to die, too."

"All right, Rob. That's enough. I'm proud of you. That must have been very difficult."

He wiped his eyes on a shirtsleeve but said nothing.

"Now I want you to relax for a minute. Close your eyes and just relax. Let your body unwind, all your fingers and toes. Good. I'd like to speak with Harry for a minute. Harry?"

No response.

"Harry, it's no use hiding. I could put Robin under hypnosis and find you that way." I wasn't so sure of this, but I hoped Harry would believe me. "Come on out. I just want to talk to you for a minute. I won't hurt you, I promise."

"You won't punish me?"

"Harry?"

His face was that of a bitter, scowling five-year-old. "I wouldn't care if you did punish me. I'd do it all over again."

"What would you do, Harry?"

"I'd kill Uncle Dave again if I got the chance." He looked mean enough to do it.

"You killed Uncle Dave?"

"Yes. Isn't that what you wanted to ask me about?"

"Well—yes. How did you kill him?"

"I broke his big fat neck."

"Where did this happen?"

"In the backyard. It was wet."

"Uncle Dave had done something to Sally and Rebecca?"

"Yes," he snarled. "The same thing he did to Robin."

"So you killed him."

"I told you I would and I did."

"Now this is very important, Harry. Did you ever kill anyone else?"

"No. Just the big fat pig."

"All right. Thank you for coming out, Harry. You can go back now. If we need you again I'll let you know."

The scowl slowly disappeared.

I waited a moment. "Rob?"

"Yes."

"Did you hear any of that?"

"Any of what?"

"Harry was just here. He told me what happened. He told me who killed the man that murdered your wife and daughter."

"*I* killed him."

"No, Rob, you never killed anyone. It was Harry who killed the intruder."

"Harry?"

"Yes."

"But Harry is only five years old, isn't he?"

"That's true, but he occupies a very strong body. Yours."

I could almost see a pair of lights come on in Robert's eyes. "You mean after all those years, I've been running from something that never happened?"

"It happened, Rob, and Sally and Rebecca are gone. But you didn't kill the man. Harry did."

"But Harry is me!"

"Yes, he's a part of you. But you are not responsible for his actions, not until he is integrated into your own personality. Do you understand?"

"I—I guess so." He looked puzzled.

"And there's another problem. You blamed yourself for their deaths because you had gone to work that Saturday instead of staying home with them."

"It was a nice day. They wanted me to take the day off."

"Yes."

"But I didn't because we needed the overtime pay."

"Yes, Rob. You went in that Saturday like all the rest of

your fellow workers. Do you understand? Nothing that happened that day was your fault. None of it."

"But Sally and Becky died because I wasn't there."

"That's true, Rob, and we can't bring them back. But I think you're ready to face that now, don't you?"

His chest rose and fell, rose and fell. "I guess it's time to go on with things."

"It's time to begin the final phase of your treatment."

"The integration."

"Yes."

He thought about this, collected himself. "How do we do that?" He absentmindedly grabbed a banana and began peeling it.

"The first thing we do is get you to stay around as much as possible. I want you to be Robert from now on unless I specifically ask one of the others to come out."

"I don't know if I can keep prot in."

"We'll take it a day at a time. Just do your best."

"I'll try."

"From now on the entire hospital is your safe haven. Understand?"

"I understand," he said.

"C'mon—I'll go back to Ward Two with you."

It was with a profound sense of sadness that I learned that Emma Villers had been diagnosed with an untreatable and rapidly progressing form of pancreatic cancer.

I knew something must have gone terribly wrong when Klaus appeared in my office after the session with Robert, staring and ashen. I thought it was he who was ill, and I asked him to sit down. He shook his head and blurted out the whole story. "She vas afraid of doctors," he said. "She neffer vent and I neffer made her." Pulling himself together, he added, "I am taking a leaf of absence. Vile I am gone you vill be acting director."

I started to protest—I had thought all that minutiae was behind me—but how could I? He looked so forlorn that I pounded him on the shoulder (a first for both of us) and told him not to worry about the hospital. He gave me the keys to his office, I expressed some feeble condolences and encouragement about his wife's condition, and he went away, his rounded shoulders drooping more than ever. Suddenly I remembered Russell's preaching the rapidly approaching apocalypse, and I realized, finally, what he meant: For him, for anyone, dying meant the end of the world.

I sat down and tried to get a fix on these unwelcome developments. But all I could think of was gratitude and relief that it wasn't my own wife or one of my children, and I vowed to spend more time with Karen and to call my sons and daughters more often. Then I remembered that as acting director I would have even less time than before, and I reluctantly headed for Villers's office hoping to find his desk cleaned off as, indeed, it usually is. Instead, it was much like my own, covered with unanswered letters, unreviewed papers, unattended messages and memos. His calendar was filled from eight-thirty to four-thirty or later every day for weeks ahead. And I thought, with mixed emotions: Retirement will have to wait.

On the train home that evening I pondered Rob's rapid progress and where to go from here. It had all happened so fast, so unexpectedly, that I hadn't thought much about his treatment once he was out of his protective shell. On top of that, I had to do Klaus's job as well as my own. I knew I was in for another sleepless night.

I struck up a conversation with a fellow traveler, who had spent the afternoon with his father, a recent heart-attack victim. I told him that a coworker of mine had taken some time off to be with his dying wife. He sympathized completely, relating all the good things about his marriage of six years, how much he would miss his wife if anything happened to her. Turned out he had been married three times already and was on his way to spend the weekend with his mistress, whom, he claimed, he also loved dearly.

I thought: Not for me. In thirty-six years of marriage I have never been unfaithful to Karen. Not even *before* we were married (we were childhood sweethearts). It's not that I possess an unusual degree of loyalty, nor am I any kind of saint. The fact is, I'd be a damn fool to do anything to lose her. At that moment I fervently hoped she would get her wish and we could retire soon to some wonderful place in the country.

Then I remembered Frankie, who would never know the bliss of love and marriage. I felt as sorry for her as I did for Klaus and Emma Villers. Frankie had been Klaus's patient, and now she was my responsibility. I vowed right then to do whatever I could to get to the bottom of her problem, to put a little joy into her sad, loveless life.

Over the weekend Will broke the code. To be certain he was right, he had run through several of Dustin's recorded "statements," and they all checked out. Will was now the only person in the world (except for prot, presumably) who could figure out what Dustin was saying.

He called me from the hospital on Sunday afternoon, as excited as I had ever heard him. "Prot was right—it was the carrot!"

"What do carrots have to do with Dustin's gibberish?"

"It's not gibberish. It's like a game with him. He sees everything in terms of roots—square roots, cube roots, and so on. There's no limit. He's a kind of savant!"

Looking back on it, I suppose I should have been more thrilled about Will's discovery. When I didn't reply, he exclaimed, "Remember that thing we worked on a few weeks ago—'Your life sure is fun . . .' and so on? The carrot is a root, see, and the four chomps on it make it a quadruple root thing: the second, fourth, eighth, and sixteenth word of the sentence, and the cycle repeats itself four times. All of his other statements are variations on that theme, depending on how many repeats and how many bites of the carrot. Get it?"

"I'm very proud of you, son. That was quite an accomplishment."

"Thanks, Pop. I'll come in some time soon and we'll talk about whether anything can be done for Dustin. I have some ideas on that."

"Really? I'd like to hear them."

"It's his parents."

"How so?"

"I think they're the problem. His father, anyway. I came in several evenings and watched them when they were together. Did you ever notice how he tries to compete with Dustin all the time? It's the only way they can communicate. At home all they did was play games. All his life Dustin has been smothered by trying to compete with his father, a game he couldn't possibly win. Don't you see? He had to devise something his old man couldn't beat him at. I've got to run, Pop. I'll come to see you in a couple of days and we'll talk about it—okay?"

"Okay, but we're not going out for lunch!"

"Whatever you say."

"Will—did you see prot today?"

"Nope. I ran into Robert once. He remembered me. But I haven't seen prot at all. Is he gone, Dad?"

"Not yet. But soon, I think."

SESSION TWENTY-NINE

I almost called you at home yesterday," Giselle blustered as she paced around my office.

I was trying to find the paper I still hadn't reviewed, to send it back with apologies. "What's the matter now?" I asked irritably, wondering what had stopped her.

"Where's prot? What have you done with him?"

"What—he's disappeared again?"

"Nobody has seen him since Friday."

"Robert, too?"

"No, *he's* around, but prot's gone."

"Oh. I don't think he's gone back to K-PAX, if that's what you're worried about."

"He might as well have."

"Giselle, you knew he wouldn't be here forever. He must have told you that."

"But he told me he wouldn't go without letting me know."

"Me, too. That's why I don't think he's gone."

"But it's more than that. When I saw him on Friday he seemed—I don't know—*different*. Preoccupied or something. He just wasn't his old self."

"It doesn't always happen that way, but I'm not surprised to hear it."

She plopped down in the vinyl chair. "He's dying, isn't he?"

Her disconsolation softened my irritability. "It isn't like that, Giselle. What's happening, I think, is that he's slowly becoming integrated into Robert's personality. In other words, you still have him. You'll have both of them."

"You mean Robert will become more like him?"

"A bit more like him, perhaps."

"I understand what you're saying. But it's still hard to believe."

"It's hard for Rob to believe, too."

"Either way, you're going to have a difficult time explaining it to the patients. They combed the hospital yesterday looking for him."

"What do they think when they see Robert?"

"They see a fellow patient. But they don't see prot."

"Maybe they will eventually."

"I doubt it."

"That reminds me of the favor I requested of you—remember?"

"You mean to make friends with Robert, and all of that?"

"That's right. It's very important."

She looked at her hands for a long time. "We're already friends. In fact, I like him a lot. It's just that he's not prot."

"Part of him is. Will you continue to cultivate that friendship?"

She turned away for a long moment. Finally she said, "I'll do what I can."

"Thank you, Giselle. I need all the help I can get. I'm counting on you."

She nodded and got up to leave. At the door she whirled around. "What about the cetologist? I promised him that prot—"

"Trust me. It'll be all right."

"Okay, Doctor B. I'm counting on you, too."

By a show of hands I was confirmed as acting director. No one else wanted the job, not even Thorstein, at least not on a temporary basis and with the worms crawling out of the can. The remainder of the meeting was spent dividing up Villers's few patients for the duration of his absence. I took Jerry and Frankie. And Cassandra, not because I saw a fortune in milking her for predictions, but because I didn't want anyone else to be tempted. There were some objections to this, but as acting director I was able to over-rule them.

This was followed by a brief discussion of upcoming events: visits by the cetologist and the famous TV "folk psychiatrist," as well as prot's own television appearance. Goldfarb remarked that he seemed to be disappearing like a Cheshire cat, and questioned (again) whether he could be counted on to show up for the interview. I tried to calm those fears by disclosing that I was planning to try to get us out of that commitment, and that seemed to end the matter, at least for the time being.

As the conversation turned to matters of great golf games and mellow Merlots, I gazed at former patient "Catherine Deneuve"'s perfect copy of Van Gogh's *Sunflowers* and pretended I was a bee buzzing around the back forty, able to see the flowers and grass and trees in astonishing vividness, much as prot seemed to be able to do. I wondered what bees thought about. The only thing that came to mind was what Hamlet said to Horatio: "There are more things in heaven and earth than are dreamt of in your philosophy. . . ."

I decided to treat Rob as if he were a boy who was more or less ignorant about sexual matters, as indeed he was. I would explain the process to him in general terms and, if I thought he could handle it, show him some videotapes that would fill in the details. In short, I was going to have to be his surrogate father, the father he never really had.

This was not an entirely unfamiliar situation. Many times a psychiatrist must play the role of parent to a patient whose experiences with his own father or mother have been disastrous. Indeed, it would not be an exaggeration to say that many analysts are the foster heads of some very large families.

Rob came in for his twenty-ninth session a couple of hours earlier than usual, as I had requested. He seemed relatively cheerful and relaxed. We chatted for a few minutes about the weekend, which he was happy to discuss in great detail. Being in the wards on his own was a new and pleasant experience for him.

"But some of the patients don't seem to like me very much," he lamented.

"Give them time," I assured him. "They'll come around."

"I hope so."

"We're going to do something a little different today, Rob."

His demeanor changed instantly. "I thought we were through with all that."

"No hypnosis today, Rob."

A sigh of relief.

"Today the subject is sex."

His reaction was perfectly normal: "Oh. Okay."

"I'm going to give you the fundamentals, then I've got some videotapes for you to watch."

He reached for an apple, his only sign of nervousness.

I explained the basic features to him. Of course he knew what I was talking about, having been exposed to the subject throughout his school years and beyond. I merely wanted to make sure there was no misunderstanding, and to observe him as we discussed the matter. He dealt with it quite well. Although he rarely looked me in the eye, neither did he seem apprehensive.

When I had finished my exposition, I pointed to the television set I had conscripted for the occasion. "I've brought in some of the tapes we have on the subject. This will give you a far better idea of what we're talking about than anything I can tell you. I think you're ready to fill in the rest of the gaps. What do you think?"

"I guess I could give it a try."

"I warn you: These are quite explicit. X-rated. Do you understand?"

"Yes."

I studied him for any change in demeanor. There was none. "If you feel any discomfort at all, just turn it off and come and get me. I'll be right next door in my office. Okay?"

"Okay."

"Good. Do you know how to run a VCR?"

"Yes. Dustin showed me."

"Dustin? No kidding. All right. You're on your own. I've got some phone calls to make. No one will bother you." I waited for that to sink in. "See the clock behind you? I'll be back at five." I left him alone to study them in whatever way he found most informative.

I was on the phone for the next several hours canceling as many of Villers's meetings and appointments and speeches as I could get away with, and trying to fit some of the others into my own crowded schedule. I also called the hospital's chief attorney, hoping to get prot out of the TV appearance. It was too late. The papers had been signed, and there was nothing left but to go ahead with it or face a lawsuit for breach of contract. After that I spent some time shuffling things around on my desk, moving piles from here to there and back again. When five o'clock finally came I tapped on the door of my examining room.

Someone yelled, "Come in!"

I found Robert slouched down in his chair, exactly as I had left him. "How are you doing?"

He was watching a film on foreplay. "Fine," he answered, without looking up. I was pleased to see it was still Rob.

"Good. That's enough for today, I think. Would you like to see some of these again sometime?"

"It doesn't seem very complicated," he replied ingenuously. "I think I'm ready to try it on my own."

I said, quietly, "I think we can manage to find someone to help you." To myself I shouted, "Right on!"

Abby phoned us at home that evening. Karen took the call. After catching up on our various activities, Rain and Star came on. They wanted to talk to me. A new word had cropped into their vocabulary. For example, I opined that "the Giants are going all the way this year."

"That's bullshit, Grandpa." In fact, everything I said was "bullshit."

I asked to speak with their mother.

"Sure they say 'bullshit' once in a while," she sighed. "So what?"

"They're too young for that. It gives a bad impression."

"Dad, lots of yuppie kids keep their hair neatly trimmed and wear ties and watch what they say, and they couldn't give a good goddamn about their planet or the animals they share it with. Which would you rather have for a grandson?"

"I've met some very nice yuppies."

"Oh, Dad, you're impossible. But I love you anyway. Here's Steve. He wants to tell you something."

"Hello, Steve. What's up?"

"Ah just thought you'd like to know"—his chortle sounded a bit like that of a chimpanzee—"that Charlie Flynn broke his big toe this afternoon."

"What's so funny about that?"

"He had hauled some high-intensity spotlights up into the big telescope and was trying to shine them down onto the mirror. Danged if he didn't fall off."

"Why was he doing that?"

"Light-travel," he said, giggling. "He was tryin' to get to K-PAX!"

Before hanging up we chatted a while about how absentminded scientists can be. "For example," he related, "a plumber came into the department the other day to fix a clogged sink. He took off the trap underneath, caught the dirty water in a bucket, and handed it out to one of the graduate students standin' there. He said, 'Here—get rid of this.' The kid promptly dumped the water right back into the sink!" It sounded like a whole barrel of monkeys on the other end of the phone.

As soon as we finished our conversation and I dropped the receiver down, the phone rang again. It was the head night nurse. Her voice was shaking. "Dr. Brewer?"

"Yes?"

"Dr. Brewer, you're not going to believe this."

"Believe what?"

"I don't know how to begin."

"Jane! What is it?"

"Lou just had a baby!"

"You're kidding!"

"I told you you wouldn't believe it."

"Where is he now?"

"In the infirmary. Dr. Chakraborty says he and the baby are doing fine. It's a girl. Six pounds eight ounces. Seventeen inches." I could almost see the woman grinning. When she does that, her eyes almost disappear.

"But—but—when did it happen? *How* did it happen?"

"No one knows. Except prot."

"Prot? What did he have to do with it?"

"He delivered the baby."

My head was swimming. Did prot somehow find an abandoned child somewhere and bring it in without being seen? "All right, Jane. Thank you. I'll speak to prot and Dr. Chak in the morning."

"She's a beautiful baby," was all she had to add.

Still reeling from the news, I came in early the next morning to see Lou's impossible child for myself. I still felt it had to be some trick of prot's. But when I got to the hospital I found a big truck parked on Amsterdam Avenue. I had forgotten that Giselle's cetologist friend was coming.

In the trailer was a dolphin he wanted prot to speak to. I wasn't sure, however, that prot would be available, despite his sudden reappearance last evening. In fact, it was Robert who came out of the building and greeted me and the other patients milling around the grounds. Giselle was with him.

She introduced me to the marine biologist, a tanned young man in jeans and a T-shirt bearing a great blue whale and the phrase "Cetaceans Unlimited." He couldn't wait to get started.

"Are you going to speak to the dolphin, Rob?"

"You know I can't go outside, Dr. Brewer."

"Just wondered whether you were planning to try."

"Not quite yet." In fact, as soon as we got to the big

wrought-iron gate, prot flipped on his dark glasses and chirped, "Hi, Giselle. Got something for you." He gave her a handwritten version of his conversation with the zoo animals. "Hiya, gino. How are things?"

I said, "Prot, where did you get that baby?"

"She came from Lou. Pretty shitty delivery, doc. I told you it should've been a cesarean. Now, if you'll excuse me. . . ."

I was flabbergasted by this glib remark, but I followed him into the trailer without a word. For once I didn't want to miss anything. I left Betty to try to explain to the patients why everybody couldn't climb aboard.

The tank was big enough for the dolphin to swim around in a tight oval, but not much else. As soon as I was inside I heard prot whooping some kind of call. The dolphin swam faster and began to make sounds of his own. There were lesions on his skin, perhaps from some kind of infection. Suddenly it stopped and faced prot directly. Giselle leaned over the top of the tank and watched with a huge smile; I stood a little farther away. The cetologist scrambled to get his recording equipment going. I wished I had thought to invite Abby to see this.

The conversation, or whatever it was, continued for several minutes. The pattern of sound was not regular, but varied in pitch and duration as does the dialogue between two human beings. At the end of the whole thing the dolphin, whose name, according to the hand-painted sign stuck to the side of the tank, was "Moby," uttered a pathetic wail, as if his heart were breaking.

Suddenly it was silent, except for the sounds still echoing around and around the trailer. Prot leaned over and offered his face to the dolphin, who licked it. The cetologist said, "I've tried to get him to do that for months." Prot, in turn, licked the dolphin's snout. He then wailed something of his own before jumping down and heading for the door.

"Wait!" shouted the scientist. "Aren't you going to tell me what he said?"

Prot stopped and turned around. "Nope."

"Why not?"

"You have the tapes. You figure it out."

"But I don't have anything to go on. Giselle, you told me he'd cooperate. Talk to him!"

She shrugged.

Prot turned and said, "I'll tell you what. If you quit 'studying' him and put him back in the ocean, and get all the others to do the same, I'll tell you everything he said to me."

"Please! Give me something—anything!"

"*Sacré bleu!* All right—I'll give you a hint. What he's expressing is almost pure emotion. Unabashed joy, high excitement, terrible sorrow—things you humans have forgotten about, even your children. Are you blind and deaf? He's in pain. He wants to go home. Is that such an alien concept?" He marched out of the trailer, presumably to tell the patients what he and the dolphin had been talking about.

The youthful scientist, looking like a would-be prince who had been given three impossible tasks to complete, glumly watched him leave. He whimpered, "I wanted to ask him why so many of them are beaching themselves lately." All I could do was shrug, too. The dolphin, I noticed, was staring at us.

But it was Robert, not prot, who joined the patients waiting outside. Yet, when he headed off toward Adonis, some of them trailed after him! Was it Robert or prot they were following? Or someone in-between?

As I was going up the walk I heard a familiar patter behind me. Giselle caught up. "I've been thinking about what you said."

"And?"

"And I think you're right. Rob is a lot like prot."

"I'm glad you feel that way."

"And even if you're wrong," she added, "I think he needs me."

"We both do," I assured her as I hurried off to the clinic to see Lou.

I found Chakraborty poring over some sonograms and X-rays. "What do you make of it?" I asked him.

"According to the pictures, he has a uterus and one small ovary. They are connected with the rectum." There were stars in his eyes. "I have not seen anything ever like it."

"Prot has always told me we should listen more to what our patients are saying to us. After this, I'm inclined to agree. How soon can he leave here?"

"He is okay to go away in one day. Should I send him back to Ward Number Two?"

"That's up to Beamish. I'll speak to him. Let's go see Lou."

"One final thing. I am very sorry to tell you, but I took a call from the big hospital one moment ago. Russell has died. Do you want them to bring him back here? After the autopsy, of course."

I had been expecting this news, but I was nonetheless stunned. I had known Russell for many years. He was a nuisance, a pain in the neck sometimes, but I had gotten used to having him around, and so had the rest of the staff and patients. In a peculiar way, he was a sincere and good friend to all of us. Yet, only Maria, a former MPI patient who had become a nun, was with him when he died. "Yes, have them send him back here. We'll bury him on the back forty."

"I think he would be liking that very much."

Lou was sitting up drinking some apple juice. One of the nurses was nearby feeding the baby from a bottle. I shook my head in wonder. "She's a pretty little girl, Lou. Have you decided on a name for her yet?"

"When I first got here, the other patients and I decided to call her 'Protista.' "

SESSION THIRTY

Giselle, with the help of a city employee she knew, learned that Bert had impregnated his girlfriend while they were in high school. Without his knowledge, the girl had sought an abortion from a neighborhood quack and, unfortunately, had died in the makeshift "clinic." When Bert found out about this, he was devastated to the extent that he never went out with a woman again.

But it wasn't until thirty years later that his mother paid an unexpected visit and found his closet full of dolls and children's clothing, a futile attempt to resurrect his lost daughter. Her discovery precipitated a chain of events that led to his violent eruption and hospitalization, where vigorous treatment with a variety of antidepressant drugs failed to relieve Bert of his all-pervasive sense of loss, and he finally ended up at MPI.

Armed with these facts, I went to see him. I found him in the lounge helping Jackie build a Lego house. Frankie was there, too, her great bulk perched precariously on the window ledge. She was staring morosely out the big window, ignoring all of us.

I found a chair and pulled it up to watch the construction project. Jackie was as involved, carefree, and happy as any nine-year-old, while Bert played the role of father, praising the laying of every new brick, not interfering unless something went awry.

"I know about your daughter," I told him.

He continued to help Jackie with her new house.

"You must miss her very much."

He pretended not to hear me.

"I have an idea you might like."

He glanced briefly in my direction, then helped Jackie figure out how to position a double window.

"Jackie needs a father. You need a daughter. How would you like to 'adopt' her? Not legally, of course—there are certain problems with that. Unofficially."

He looked at me with a pathetic appeal. But he didn't, or was unable to, say anything. Jackie added another brick to the little house. Bert's chin began to flutter.

I patted him on the shoulder and left him to contemplate the possibilities while I ambled over to talk with Frankie. She, too, was preoccupied with other matters and seemed not even to notice that I had taken a seat beside her on the sill, where Howie had once planted himself to search for the "bluebird of happiness."

"I've been talking to prot," I told her.

"Where is he?" she demanded, without looking at me. "What have you bastards done with him?"

"He isn't far away. He explained everything to me."

214

Frankie fixed a steely gaze on me. "Have you ever thought about doing something about your obnoxious voice?"

"You're unable to love anyone for the same reason he is. You find it irrelevant. It seems stupid to focus your feelings on one single person and forget about everyone else. Am I getting warm?"

She stared at me for another long moment. "I may puke," she said.

"Go ahead and puke, but hear me out first. No one you have ever met has any concept of how you feel, and even when you explain it they still don't get it. In fact, they think you're crazy. And worse, heartless. Am I right?"

"Did you know your nose would choke a horse?"

"I'll be perfectly honest with you. I find it hard to understand how you can be indifferent toward other people. It seems unnatural to me. But I'm beginning to see how *you* can feel that way, thanks to prot. Can we work together? Maybe we can learn something from each other."

She threw back her head and brayed like a donkey.

I was extremely pleased to see how confident Rob had become. He was at ease with Giselle, the patients, the staff. Indeed, when he came into my examining room he grabbed my hand and shook it.

At the same time, I wondered whether he had made such good progress that he might suddenly find himself facing the TV cameras during prot's talk-show appearance. I didn't want to think about the consequences that might result from such a situation.

Thus, I spent a good part of the morning trying to reverse what I had worked so hard to accomplish over the past few weeks and years, i.e., explain to Robert why he should stay in the background while prot was doing the television interview. He reminded me that he was quite content to remain in the hospital, his safe haven, and leave the rest of the world to prot, at least for the time being.

The other problem was getting prot, who was showing up less and less often, to come out and do the show. But he had said he would do the "gig" (as he called it), and with prot, a promise is a promise.

"You want to see some more tapes, Rob? Or are you bored with them?"

"Not exactly, but—"

"I've asked Giselle if she would like to see them, too. Would you be interested in having some company while you watch?"

His smile was faintly reminiscent of prot's, though the latter wouldn't have had the slightest interest in the films. "I'm willing if she is," he replied.

I called her out of my office, where she had been waiting. (I should mention here that Giselle and I had discussed the desirability of using condoms, should the need arise. In response she had pulled a couple from her pocket and waved them at me.) Now, I was surprised to find, she was actually blushing. Rob took her hand and led her to the sofa I had brought in.

I went back to my office and locked the door with a loud click, leaving them to their own devices, nature to take its course.

Prot seemed rather pensive during the limo ride to the television studio. He didn't even remark on all the noise and trash along the way or the state-of-the-art gizmos he found in the back of the car—the bar, the quad stereo system, the refrigerator stocked with food. Perhaps he was thinking about what he might say to the cameras. Or maybe he was uncomfortable with the new suit we had bought for him. Giselle and the security guards were quiet, too, all three of them staring blankly out the one-way windows at the passersby trying to peer in.

"Prot?"

"Hmmmmm?"

"I just wanted you to know that I had nothing to do with this."

"Sure, coach. I understand perfectly."

"But now that you're going through with it, I'd like to give you some advice."

"Give away."

"If I were you I wouldn't tell the audience they're a bunch of fools and a cancer on the Earth."

"Yes—you humans do have a difficult time with the truth."

"You could put it that way."

"You worry too much, dr. b."

"The other thing is: Please don't let Robert appear before the cameras. It could be devastating for him."

"I won't encourage him to do that, but he has a mind of his own, you know."

We were taken through a side door into the studio, where we were met by the show's producer. I'd never seen such a huge grin or more perfectly capped teeth. After some small talk, Giselle and I were shown to a little green room furnished with a couple of chairs, a table with a pot of coffee, and a great big monitor, where we were left with a very young production assistant. Prot was led away to makeup. "Good luck!" I bellowed after him. I was as nervous as the Ward Two patient we call "Don Knotts."

While we waited I asked Giselle about Rob's reaction to the sex tapes. Her smile was about as wide as that of the producer's. "We didn't watch any tapes."

"You're sure it wasn't Paul you were dealing with?"

"Positive. I could tell by his voice, for one thing. Not at all like the Paul on the tape you let me hear. It was Rob, all right. He was like a kid in a candy store."

Prot was brought on last, after the movie starlet, who appeared to have an IQ of about ten, and the male model/stripper. He was warmly welcomed when he finally came out to face the audience and the cameras, and the show's hostess, a possible manic, if not amphetamine-dependent, seemed genuinely taken with him, as are most of us who know him.

She began innocuously enough, if perhaps a bit tongue-in-cheek, by asking him about life on K-PAX, why he had come to Earth, what space travel was like, and so on. (At one point the director flashed on the screen a computerized juxtaposition of one of prot's star charts, which he had drawn for me much earlier when I was trying to determine the extent of his astronomical knowledge, with a picture of the real thing.) Most of it I had heard before. But she also asked him one or two things I should have thought of and hadn't. For example, how does one stop after traveling through interplanetary space at superlight speed? (As near as I could figure out, it's sort of programmed in.) Prot answered all the questions politely, if matter-of-factly, from behind his dark glasses. I waited for the interviewer to get to something more controversial and try to put him on the spot. At that point the band struck up a jazzy rendition of "Two Different Worlds" and there was a pause for some commercials.

I asked the production assistant whether the hoobah was decaffeinated. She gave me a strange look.

When the program returned, the hostess, winking at the camera, asked prot whether he would mind giving us a little demonstration of light-travel.

"Why not?" prot answered. Giselle and I and the assistant leaned forward in our chairs as, I assume, did most of the audience. Someone brought out a flashlight and mirror. Prot grinned. Apparently he had been expecting something like this.

In any case, he placed the light on his right shoulder and pointed it toward the mirror, which he held in his outstretched left hand. The room we were in was so quiet I could hear everyone breathing. Suddenly there was a very brief flash of light and prot disappeared from the screen! The audience gasped. The camera jostled around until it found prot on the other side of the stage standing behind the microphone reserved for singers and stand-up comics. He was wearing a funny little hat. I recognized it at once: It was Milton's. He tweaked an imaginary mustache and chirped, "Bear walks into a bar, see? Takes out a pistol and plugs everyone in the place. The cops come and take him away. 'What's wrong?' the bear protests. 'Humans ain't on the endangered species list!' "

No one laughed.

"Am I going too slow for you guys? All right—how about this one: Who are the first to line up for wars, to pull the executioner's switch, to murder all their fellow beings because they taste good? Give up? The pro-lifers!"

No one laughed.

"You're not trying, folks—who is your leader? One more time: Two Christians get married. What religion will their children adopt? I'll give you a hint. It works for Muslims and Jews and Hindus alike. . . . Nothing? Okay. See, it has to do with where people get their so-called ideas. . . ."

The audience, shaken by what they had seen, still didn't laugh. The hostess, her tongue no longer in her cheek, asked prot to return to his seat. "How—how did you do that?" she demanded.

"I learned the routine from one of my fellow inmates."

"No—I mean how did you get to the other side of the room?"

"I told you earlier—remember?"

She requested an instant replay of what she called prot's "light-and-mirrors trick" in super slow motion. But no matter how slow the motion, prot always disappeared from the screen. In our little room Giselle laughed and clapped her hands. The production assistant gaped at the monitor and said nothing. The band started up, the 800 number flashed onto the screen, and there was another pause for commercial messages.

When the show began again, the hostess, much more

serious now, brought out a prepared list of questions for prot. What follows is a verbatim transcription:

HOSTESS: You have written [she was referring to prot's "report"] that there are certain things we humans must give up in order to survive as a species. One of these is religion. Can you elaborate on that?

PROT: Certainly. Have you ever noticed that a great many of your present difficulties are based on the intolerance of one set of believers for the beliefs of others?

H: Too many, probably, and we all see your point. What I'd like you to tell us is how we give up something that's such an intrinsic part of our human nature?

P: That's entirely up to you. The evidence I've seen so far suggests you don't have the guts.

H: What do you mean by "guts"?

P: Religion is based primarily on fear. It started that way and it continues to this day.

H: Fear of what?

P: You name it.

H: You mean death.

P: That's one thing.

H: What about money?

P: What about it?

H: How can we give up money? What would we use instead?

P: For what?

H: To buy a washing machine, for example.

P: Why do you need washing machines?

H: Because they save time and energy.

P: In other words, you've flooded your planet with washing machines and cars and plastic soda bottles and tv sets so you'll have more time and energy?

H: Yes.

P: And in order to keep the economy going you need more and more human beings in order to buy more and more of your products. Am I right so far?

H: Well, growth is good for everyone.

P: Not for the several million other species on your PLANET. And what happens when your WORLD is full of people and cars and washing machines and there isn't room for any more?

[The music started up.]

Giselle and I looked at each other and shrugged. I went to the little adjoining rest room. In a moment or two I heard her yell: "Dr. B! He's back!" I hurried in to find the program's hostess holding up a small dog. It was yapping frantically.

"What's he saying?" she demanded of prot.

"He wants to take a [bleep]," prot responded. The audience, now on more familiar ground, roared. They howled even more when the dog defecated, as if on cue, on top of the big desk. The merriment went on for several minutes as the hostess mugged for the cameras, got rid of the dog, and someone came out to clean up the mess. They were still laughing when it was time for the next series of commercials.

The show returned to a smattering of titters, but this ended abruptly when the dialogue resumed.

> *H:* You seem to find a lot wrong with us humans. But you have to admit we have our good points, too. If you were to use one word to characterize our species, what would it be?
>
> [Prot's eyes rolled up for a moment—he was thinking. Like everyone else who was watching, probably, a number of things came to *my* mind: "generosity," "perseverance," "a sense of humor. . . ."]
>
> *P:* I haven't decided whether it's ignorance or just plain stupidity.
>
> *H:* And that's why you think that mankind won't make what you call the necessary decisions to survive as a species.
>
> *P:* Or womankind either.
>
> *H:* Yet there are many who think we can overcome these difficulties and win this war. Why do you think that's not possible?
>
> *P:* It's not impossible. Beings on other WORLDS have done it. But it's pretty much too late for that here. You've already begun to destroy your home. That's the beginning of the end.
>
> *H:* So what's going to happen to us, in your view?

P: You don't want to hear it.

H: I'd really like to know. How about it, audience?

[A smattering of applause.]

P: It's your funeral. All right—it will be a gradual decline at first, like cancer or aids. You won't notice much except for the disappearance of a few more nonhuman beings and the usual little wars everywhere. Fuel and mineral resources will begin to run out. Emergency meetings of nations will be held, but self-interests will prevail, as they always have, and the more desperate or greedy among you will make demands and ultimatums. These will not be met, and larger wars will break out. In the meantime your entire environmental support system will begin to collapse. There will be enormous suffering among all the inhabitants of the EARTH, even those who still possess relative wealth and power. After that, it's only a question of time. Death could come in any number of ways, but it is as certain as taxes.

[The hostess stared at him and said nothing for a moment.]

P: I told you you wouldn't want to hear it.

H: Life will just end on Earth?

P: There will still be life, but human beings will never return to this PLANET. Similar species might evolve, but the likelihood that one of them will be homo sapiens is very small. You are a rare breed in the UNIVERSE, you know. A freak of nature, so to speak.

H: And there's no way to stop this?

P: Sure. All you have to do is start over with a different set of assumptions.

H: You mean the business of eliminating money, families, religion, countries—things like that?

P: It's not really so difficult. You just have to decide whether these things are more important to you than your survival. For example— you gave up smoking, right?

[Yet another soft musical hint: "Two different worlds. . . ."]

H: Uh—yes, I did. But—

P: Was it easy?

H: It was hell.

P: But now you never miss it, do you?

[The music came up, more persistently than before.]

P: Look—why not try living without wars, religions, specieside, and all the rest for a decade or two? If you don't like it you can always go back to the hatred and killing and endless growth. . . .

H: Back after these messages.

[When the show returned, the starlet decided to get into the act. The facade of dumbness had fallen off.]

S: You forgot to factor the human spirit into your equations.

P: That's a meaningless term concocted, no doubt, by some homo sapiens or other.

S: What about Shakespeare? Mozart? Picasso? The human race has accomplished some great things, even by your standards. In fact, we humans have made this a pretty wonderful world!

[A smattering of applause.]

P [gazing at the camera with his familiar look of exasperation mixed with mild contempt]: What kind of world is it where violence and war are not only accepted, but your youth are encouraged to practice them? Where your leaders must be constantly guarded against assassination, and airline travelers frisked for weapons? Where every vial of aspirin must be protected against poisoning? Where some of your beings make fortunes to play games while others are starving? Where no one believes a single word your governments or your corporations say? Where your stockbrokers and film stars are more valued than your teachers? Where the numbers of human beings increase and increase while other species are driven to extinction? Where—

["Two different worlds. . . ."]

H: Don't go 'way. We'll be right back!

No one in the little room said anything. We all watched the commercials, thought our divergent thoughts. In a little while our hostess returned with: "We've been talking with prot, a visitor from the planet K-PAX, where things are a lot simpler than they are here on Earth. Prot, our time is up. Will you come back and visit us again?"

"Why—weren't you listening?" He was still wearing the funny hat and the suit and I didn't know which looked sillier on him.

"Good night, folks, good night! Good night!"

There was no applause. The audience, apparently, was still confused by what they had seen and heard. Or perhaps they merely figured his were the words of a crazy man.* Just before the show went off the air there was another extreme slow-motion shot of prot disappearing abruptly from view, and the 800 number flashed one final time on the screen.

---

*Some of prot's other comments, which space did not permit including here, are listed in "The Wisdom (or Craziness) of prot," at the end of this book.

When they brought him back to our little room he was grinning broadly. I stuck out my hand, as proud of him as if he were my own son. Not for what he had said, but because he had kept his word and done the show without allowing Robert to make an appearance.

"See you later, doc," he said. He turned to Giselle and whispered, "Bye, kid." She hugged him. When he stepped back it was Rob, still wearing prot's sunglasses and Milton's hat, who faced us.

I was puzzled. I hadn't expected this. Had prot decided to throw Rob into the water, to force him to sink or swim? I quickly explained the situation to him—where he was, what had happened. He looked at me with a hint of amusement, just as prot might have done. When we left the little waiting room he was happy and relaxed, which was more than could be said for me.

On the way back to the hospital he played with the gizmos, waved at the staring passersby, seemed to soak up the excitement of the city, which he had never seen. "From now on, the whole world is your safe haven," I told him, though it was obviously unnecessary. By the time we got "home" he was sound asleep, his head resting on Giselle's shoulder.

The morning after the televised interview a pair of CIA agents were in my (Villers's) office waiting for me. They demanded to speak with prot.

"I don't know where he is," I responded truthfully.

"You mean he's gone?"

"Looks that way."

They seemed dubious, but one of them suddenly came

up with a notebook and scribbled something into it. He ripped out a page and handed it to me. It was a beeper number. "If he shows up again, let us know right away." I almost expected them to insist that I eat the message, but they whirled around simultaneously and rushed out the door, as if all hell were breaking loose somewhere.

After they had gone I went to look for Rob. I found him in his room with Giselle. Both were reading or, perhaps, studying. They looked exactly like a couple of college students preparing for exams in a co-ed dorm.

I took a look at the stack of dusty books resting on Rob's little table like old treasure chests about to be opened: *Birds of the Northeast*, *Moby Dick*, and several others. In his hands rested a recent tome by Oliver Sacks. As normal as apple pie, I thought, with no little satisfaction.

Giselle was taking notes from a book called *Unexplained Mysteries*. On the floor next to her chair was a typed manuscript, the first draft of her article about UFO's.

"How are you feeling, Rob?"

"Never felt better, doc," he assured me.

"I just stopped in to give you this," I said, handing him the tape Karen had made of the talk show. "And to ask you whether you would be willing to submit to a few simple tests during your regular session tomorrow."

"Anything you say," he replied, without even asking what kind of tests they were.

I hurried out, late for a meeting, which dragged on and on. Though it was supposed to be a discussion about plans for the new wing, no one wanted to talk about anything other than prot's TV appearance the previous evening. Having been through all of it before, I finally excused myself and returned to my office, where I called Robert's mother. Confident that Rob would be around for a while, I told her of my guarded optimism about his prognosis and invited her to visit him and see for herself. She was somewhat hesitant about traveling alone, but said she would come if "that nice young girl" (Giselle, whom she had met on her previous visit to the hospital) would go with her.

I told her I didn't think that would be a problem.

With that pleasant chore taken care of, I took a call from Betty. "Dr. Villers phoned yesterday while you were gone. He wanted to speak with prot. He said it was urgent. He called again later, but I couldn't find prot—only Robert. I suggested he talk to Cassandra. He said it was too late for that."

"It may be too late for prot, too."

"That's too bad. He sounded desperate."

All the rest of that week we were inundated with calls to the 800 number. A few of the callers pledged money to the hospital. Some had a relative or friend they wanted admitted. Several producers from other talk shows wanted prot to come on their programs "and do that trick." Most of those who telephoned, however, did not apply for admission of a loved one or contribute funds toward the new wing or make prot a job offer. Instead, they wanted to know where to call or write to him, when they would see him again, how to get to K-PAX.

A few reporters called as well, asking for prot's life story and all the rest. Unable to convince them that prot *had* no "life story," and perhaps no longer existed, I finally referred them to Giselle.

Then the letters started to pour in, thousands of them, most addressed to "prot, c/o Manhattan Psychiatric Institute, New York, NY." I didn't open any of these, but I did take a look at some of the ones addressed to "prot's keepers," or the like. Some of these called him "the devil" (as Russell had at one time), and some even threatened him with bodily harm. Others thought he was a kind of Christlike figure, "a messiah for our time," who had come to "save us from ourselves." Oddly, not one person saw him for what he really was—part of a mentally ill person who seemed to be on the road to recovery.

But prot made no appearance that week (much to Villers's great dismay). I felt somehow betrayed. If he had, in fact, "departed" this world for good, he had done so without giving us any notice, something he had assured me he would not do. Still, I couldn't help think of the last time he had "returned" to K-PAX, and the Robert he had left behind. Rob was a very different person this time, smiling and confident. Maybe that was all anyone could expect.

One of the things I would never forget about prot was his ability to communicate with the autistic patients. Perhaps that explains the dream I had the night after the talk show.

I was in what appeared to be a space capsule. I could see out some tiny windows into a shimmering blue sky. The cabin was further lit by some sort of instrument panel. It was dazzling. There were dozens of dials and computer screens, all aglow with green and amber lights.

Suddenly there was a tremendous noise and everything began to vibrate. I felt the force of gravity pulling me down and down and then, after a few minutes, the noise and vibration ceased and I was floating free, miles above the Earth, looking down at the most beautiful planet in the universe.

I was jolted by something, thrown far off course, blinded by a shadow blocking my view. The next thing I knew I was back on the launch pad, and the darkness was gone from the window. A giant head appeared. It was Jerry. He had given me a ride in his perfect model. A huge eye peered in at me, and his mouth opened in a toothy grin. It was wonderful—for a moment I understood him, understood everything!

But then I woke up and, as always, I understood nothing.

SESSION THIRTY-ONE

The visit from the nation's most popular psychologist was scheduled for Friday. His books, *Folk Psychiatry* and *Clean Up Your Mess*, have been on the best-seller lists for years. I was on the lawn waiting for Cassandra to notice me when word came that, unfortunately, some "urgent business" had come up and our guest was forced to cancel at the last minute.

For some reason this annoyed me a great deal. I blurted out to the nurse, "What an ass—well, the medical term is 'anal orifice.'"

On the positive side, this gave me some unexpected free time to catch up on a lot of paperwork. But as soon as I sat down there was a call from a Dr. Sternik, the ophthalmologist Giselle had mentioned earlier, who badly wanted to examine prot's eyes.

"Sure," I said, "go ahead. If you can find him."

• • •

The first thing I asked Rob after he sat down was what he thought of the tape of the television show starring his alter ego, prot.

He took a peach from the fruit bowl. "Weird. Very weird."

"How so?"

"It was like watching myself, only it wasn't me at all."

"As I've told you before, prot is a part of you."

"I understand that, but it's still hard to believe it."

"Have you seen him in the last couple of days?"

"Not since we left the TV studio."

"Do you know where he is?"

"Nope. Does that mean I'm ready to go home?"

"We'll see."

Someone tapped lightly on the door. "Come in, Betty! All right, Rob, I'm going to ask Betty to give you a few simple tests. For your information, these are the same ones that we gave prot five years ago. I want to compare the results, see if there are any differences, okay?"

"Sure."

"Good. And after you're through here, Betty will take you to the clinic so you can give us a blood sample. That will only take a minute. And Dr. Chakraborty wants to get an EEG, which is a simple, painless recording of your brain waves."

"Fine."

Both were smiling broadly when I left them alone. Betty loves to administer tests of any kind; Rob was happy just to be in control of himself. She and Rob would miss Russell's funeral, but Betty said she didn't like funerals—she would rather remember the decedent as he was—and Rob barely knew him, if at all.

It was raining and the service was held in the lounge. A bunch of folding chairs had been brought in and everyone was facing the open casket, which was lying on the magazine table. It was a simple pine box, which is not only the usual choice for indigent patients, but had long been Russ's own wish as well, after we declined to find him a cave with a big rock for a door.

Chaplain Green made a beautiful speech about Russell and his eternal life in heaven, filled with golden streets and singing angels, and yes, hamburgers on Saturday nights. It almost made me wish I were joining him. Then it was the turn of those who knew him best.

Some of the long-term staff stood up to say how much they would miss him, and a few of the patients paid their final respects. Even former residents Chuck and Mrs. Archer had come to add a story or two, as did Howie and Ernie, who had spent years in this institution and knew him well. For my part, what I remembered best about Russ was his in-your-face style of preaching, spouting prodigious amounts of spittle along with the Scriptures. I reminded the gathering about his early days at MPI, the days of fire and brimstone. He was something to see then, with his sandy hair blowing in the wind and his gray eyes all ablaze, and you could always depend on Russell to be around to give us God's opinion of the tiniest event. In later years he had mellowed somewhat, but he never rested in his quest for lost souls. And now, for the first time in his life, he was at peace. I stopped there, stunned for a moment by a sudden understanding of the attractiveness of suicide for some people. I only hoped that none of the patients followed the same line of thought.

After the service I mingled for a while with some of our former patients, all of whom were doing well. We discussed, with considerable nostalgia, their days at the hospital (it's strange how even a stay in a mental institution can seem like a happy time in retrospect). Chuck, especially, seemed a changed man, chatting away without the slightest comment on the odor of anyone present. But it wasn't until everyone was leaving that he said, "It was good to see prot again." Confused by his crossed eyes, perhaps, I thought for a moment he meant to say "Russell," but Mrs. A and Ernie and Maria all nodded enthusiastically.

"Hasn't changed a bit," Ernie declared.

"Was prot here?" I asked as calmly as possible.

"Didn't you see him? He was standing at the back of the crowd."

I said my good-byes and returned to my examining room. Rob and Betty were still there, busily engaged in the testing process. Thinking that maybe our former patients had generated visions of prot from the rich loam of their imaginations, I went back to my office, where I placed a call to Virginia Goldfarb.

"No," she said, "I didn't see him. Why? Was he supposed to be there?" Same for Beamish and Menninger.

I ran to the lawn and checked with several of the other patients still milling about the gravesite. All of them had seen prot.

I wanted to get away from my desk, from the hospital, from everything. But I didn't know where to go. I wandered around for a while, ending up in Villers's office, where I occupied myself with correspondence and budget matters until I got a call from our new administrator, Joe Goodrich, a nice young man and quite competent, despite his limited experience. I could tell he had something he wanted to say to me, but was having a hard time doing it. Finally he blurted, "I just got a call from the *New York Times*. Klaus Villers killed his wife and then himself. Apparently it happened last night. They want you to fax them his obituary. In fact, Dr. Villers left a note requesting that you take care of it."

I mumbled something and hung up. Though I hardly knew Klaus and Emma, I was profoundly saddened by this tragic news, and I wasn't sure why. Perhaps because it came so close after Russell's death and prot's apparent departure. Too much, too soon. I felt as if I were a spider at the bottom of a sink—no matter how much I struggled, I couldn't get out. And prot wasn't there to help me.

On Saturday I drove in and forced myself to spend the day processing those parts of Rob's tests that Betty hadn't finished. Chak had also stayed late on Friday to get the blood samples off to the lab for DNA analysis and typing, though we wouldn't get the results for several weeks. I listened to a tape of *La Bohème* while I worked up the data. But I didn't sing along or even hear much of it.

At first I didn't believe the results, but I soon remembered that nothing about the case of Robert/prot could ever be routine. Here are the comparisons of some of Rob's tests with those of prot, examined five years earlier:

TEST	ROB	PROT
IQ	130	154
Short-term memory	good	excellent
Reading skill	average	very good
Artistic ability	above average	variable
Musical ability	fair	below average
General knowledge	limited	broad and impressive
Hearing, taste, smell, tactile acuities	normal	highly sensitive
"Special" senses	none	questionable
EEG	normal (though somewhat different from prot's)	normal
Vision		
1. Light sensitivity	normal	marked
2. Range	normal	can detect light well into UV range
Aptitude	some affinity for natural sciences	could do almost anything

In addition to the above, there were also slight differences in skin tone (fairness) and voice timbre. Robert and prot were two completely different people occupying the same body like a pair of Siamese twins.

As I looked over the data something kept flitting around my mind like a trapped butterfly trying to escape. Was it guilt about Klaus's death? Finally, out flew an old adage with dull brown wings: Be suspicious of the patient who discharges himself, as Robert had begun hinting we should consider for him.

Will came into my office just as I was packing up to leave for what was left of the weekend. He wanted to talk about Dustin's parents. I reminded him to finish his studies before he began his practice. But suddenly I felt a compelling need to confess my feelings of guilt about Klaus and Emma Villers. If I had tried to cultivate a friendship with him, I told Will, get to know him as well as some of his patients seemed to, maybe I could have done something. He listened intently to the whole thing, and when I was finished he said, "Sometimes you can't do anything about a problem no matter how hard you try."

"Son, I think you've got the makings of a fine shrink."

"Thanks, Pop. Now, what about Dustin's parents?"

I sighed, "Don't worry—I'll take care of it."

"I wonder if parents aren't the cause of half the mental problems in the world," he mused.

"Damn near," I sighed. "Prot would probably say we ought to do away with parenthood altogether."

SESSION THIRTY-TWO

The Monday-morning staff meeting began with a moment of silence for our departed colleague. After that I discussed my misgivings about Rob. By now everyone was aware that he was making excellent progress, and that there had been no appearances by prot (except, perhaps, to the patients at Russell's funeral) for several days. Someone asked whether Robert, who showed no signs of psychosis whatever, wouldn't do just as well in Ward One. I demurred: "Let's wait to hear from Virginia and Carl" (Goldfarb and Thorstein were absent for Rosh Hoshanah).

Perhaps I was being overly cautious. I suppose everyone becomes more conservative as he gets older. I had, after all, been wary about Michael, who was doing very well as an EMS trainee, despite the fact that he had attempted suicide as recently as a few months earlier. And, thanks mainly to prot, Rudolph was also gone, Manuel was on the verge of departure, Lou had gotten through a very difficult delivery, and now Bert was making excellent progress as well. Maybe he had worked similar wonders with Rob.

After the brief meeting I went to see Bert, who unburdened himself of the whole story. After his girlfriend's death, their unborn child kept growing and growing in his head like a kind of mental fetus. The headaches were excruciating. He kept everything bottled up inside for years, until he was well past forty, when his mother's serendipitous discovery eventually triggered the cascade of events that sent him to us.

This is not unusual. Many nervous or other mental breakdowns result from a sudden eruption, like a geyser, of feelings long repressed. Most of us have something locked up inside, trying to break out. One of my former teachers once remarked that if science could find some way for the brain to let off this steam, a little at a time, there would be far less mental trauma in the world, and certainly in the hospitals. Unfortunately, so little attention is paid to mental health, even as part of a regular medical checkup, that such a goal has yet to be attained.

Bert told me how he had bought dolls and clothes and spent nearly every night of his adult life bathing his "daughter" (he had arbitrarily chosen the sex of the baby), and putting her to bed, taking care of her when she was "sick," and all the rest. When he was finished, and the tears were over, I asked him again about adopting Jackie. By this time, the other patients had stopped whatever they were doing and drifted over to listen, and we all waited for the answer.

"It would be the happiest day of my life," Bert blubbered, and I had no trouble believing him.

At that moment I heard something I had never heard in over thirty years of practice. The small group of patients that had gathered nearby broke into spontaneous applause. For a second I thought they were thanking me. But of course it was Bert (and prot) they were lauding, and I happily joined them.

Inflated with borrowed success, I headed for 3B. On the way there I thought hard about what prot had said and done to get Jerry to respond to him. It seemed simple enough—he just held his hand and gently stroked it, almost as if it were a bird or some small animal he was trying to calm.

I closed the door and eased over to where Jerry was finishing his replica of the space shuttle, complete with launch pad. Not wishing to disturb him, I crept closer.

I watched for a while, marveling at the detail, the obvious understanding of structure and function, a Michelangelo of the matchstick. At the same time, I remembered prot's comment to me about the model: "The space shuttle program is like Columbus sailing up and down the coast of Portugal."

I said, "Hello, Jerry."

"Hello, Jerry."

"Jerry, would you come with me for a moment, please?"

He froze, a sculpture in flesh and bone. Even his cowlicks seemed to become more rigid. I couldn't see his eyes, but I imagined their suspicion and fear.

"I'm not going to hurt you. I just want to talk to you for a minute."

I tugged him patiently to a chair. After a little encouragement he sat down, though now he could barely keep still. I pulled up another. Taking his hand in mine I began stroking it and speaking to him gently, as prot had done, or seemed to. I'm not sure precisely what I expected. I *hoped* he would leap up and shout, "Hiya, doc, how's it going?" or some such thing. But he never looked in my direction, never made a sound, but continued to fidget and fitfully scan the walls and ceiling.

I wouldn't give up. Like a paramedic who works over a dying patient for an hour or more, I continued to stroke Jerry's hand and arm and speak softly to him. I varied the pressure, the cadence, switched from one hand to the other—nothing worked. After that hour I was exhausted, sweating as though we had been arm wrestling the whole time. "Okay, Jerry, you can go back to work."

Without so much as a glance he jumped up and returned to his model. I could hear him muttering, "Back to work, back to work, back to work. . . ."

I decided, before lunch, to find and inform all of Klaus's patients of his death and to tell them who their new therapist would be. There was no need. All of them had heard about the tragedy and knew about the changes. What surprised me was the depth of feeling they expressed for their former counselor. In fact, they loved my longtime colleague, obviously much more than had I or the rest of the staff.

But, of course, I never had a session with Klaus. The bonds between a patient and his psychiatrist are strong, often resembling, as I have said, that of a parent and child.

In Villers's case it appeared to be even stronger than that. From what I gathered he spent as much time telling them about his problems as vice versa. In so doing, he broke the first rule of psychiatry. But what he lost in effectiveness, if anything, he made up for in the affection his patients held for him, and their willingness to try to please him. I wished I had made a greater effort to get to know him better myself.

As long as I was in Ward Two I decided to have lunch there. The patients, even those who had little contact with Villers, seemed strangely quiet during the meal. I noticed that they kept staring at Rob, who looked like prot but wasn't exactly him. They still came to him for help on occasion and he was perfectly willing to give it. Whether he was as effective as prot in some of his advice remained to be determined.

All of this might have been moot, however. I had nearly decided to transfer him to Ward One to see how he would deal with the change. But, assuming he did well, what would the other patients think about both of them leaving the hospital for good? One of the favorite terms now being bandied about the hospital was "anal orifice." Would they think I was a first-class orifice for letting Robert/prot go?

While I was in Two, my temporary administrative secretary had taken a message, which she later passed on to me, from Klaus's lawyer. There was to be no formal burial service for him and his wife, only a simple cremation. They had requested that I scatter the ashes around Emma's flower garden. I was touched by this entreaty and, of course, agreed to it.

It was with a certain amount of wistfulness that I welcomed Rob to his last regularly scheduled session with me. I knew I would miss him, and I most certainly would miss prot, with whom I had spent even more time, and from whom I had learned a great deal. But of course I was nonetheless happy with the way things had turned out.

"Well, Rob, how are you feeling today?" I began.

"Fine, Doctor B. How about yourself?"

"A little dragged out, I'm afraid."

"You've been working too hard lately. You should slow down."

"Easy for you to say."

"I suppose so." He looked around. "Got any fruit? I seem to have developed a taste for it."

"Sorry. I forgot."

"That's okay. Maybe next time."

"Rob, at this moment you seem perfectly fine to me. Do you think you are well?"

"I've been asking myself the same question. I'm a lot better, that's for sure."

"Hear anything from prot?"

"No. I really think he's gone."

"Does that bother you?"

"Not really. I don't think we need him anymore."

"Rob?"

"Yes?"

"I'd like to hypnotize you one last time. Do you mind?"

He seemed studiously unperturbed. "I suppose not. But why?"

"I'd just like to see whether I can call up prot. It won't take long."

"Okay. Sure. Let's get it over with."

"Fine. Just focus your attention on the little dot. . . ."

He did so without the usual struggle. When he was in a deep trance I said, abruptly, "Hello, prot. I haven't seen you in a while."

There was no response except, perhaps, for a barely perceptible grin. I tried again. And again. I knew he had to be in there somewhere. But, if so, he wasn't about to come out.

After I had awakened Rob I said, "I think you're right. For all practical purposes, he's gone."

"I think so, too."

I studied him carefully. "How do you feel about my transferring you to Ward One?"

"I'd like that very much."

"I might be able to get the assignment committee's approval by tomorrow morning. Are you sure you can handle it?"

"The sooner the better."

"I'm glad you feel that way. Tell me—what do you plan to do with your life once you escape our clutches?"

He pondered the question, but not like prot would have contemplated it, his eyes focused on the ceiling or rolled up into his head. Rob simply frowned. "Well, I thought I would start by taking a trip to Guelph. See some old friends, visit Sally's and Becky's graves, the school I went to, the house I lived in. After that, I'd like to try to get into a college. It's probably too late for this year. Maybe next. Giselle is all in favor of that."

"Do you want to talk a little about your relationship with Giselle?"

"I like Giselle very much. She's not as pretty as Sally was, but she's smarter, I think. She's the most interesting person I've ever met, except for prot. That's one of the reasons I want to go back home. To say good-bye to Sally and kind of get her permission to be with Giselle. I think she would have understood."

"I'm sure she would have. Bear in mind, though, that it might be a while before you can make the trip. I may want to keep you in Ward One for a few weeks. Just to make sure there aren't any problems we've missed."

"If I'm good, do I get time off for good behavior?"

"Maybe."

"Then I'll be very good."

"You really want to get out of here, don't you?"

"Wouldn't you?"

"Yes, of course. I just wanted to hear you say it."

"I've been here more than five years. That's enough, don't you think?"

"Plenty." I glanced at my pad. "Rob, there's one more thing that has bothered me all this time, but I didn't want to ask you until you were well enough."

"What is it?"

"Prot claimed he left for a few days in 1990 to visit Iceland, Greenland, Newfoundland, and Labrador. You remember that from the tapes?"

"Yes."

"Did you go with him?"

"No, I didn't."

"Nobody saw you during that time. Where were you?"

"I hid in the storage tunnel."

"Why?"

"I wasn't ready to face anyone alone."

"Prot told you to go there?"

"No, he just gave me the key. He said, 'The rest is up to you.'"

"All right, Rob. Anything else you want to tell me before you go back to the wards?"

He thought some more. "Just one thing."

"What's that?"

"I want to thank you for all you've done for me."

"Psychiatric treatment is like a marriage, Rob—it takes a tremendous effort from both parties. You should give yourself most of the credit."

"All the same, thank you."

This time I offered him *my* hand. When he took it he looked me straight in the eye. He seemed as sane as any human being could ever be.

The following morning Lou and her daughter were discharged. I've never seen a happier mother or a more beautiful child. When she left she promised to stop by again soon. "But first," she said, "I'm going to have a sex-change operation."

"I think that would be a very good idea."

She waved as she carried Protista out the gate. Although technically she was Beamish's patient, I somehow felt the loss of another daughter separating the ties.

• • •

On Thursday, September 28, three of Klaus's patients and I spread the Villerses' combined ashes around Emma's beautiful flower garden at their Long Island home. At last the tears came, for all of us.

That afternoon, exactly six weeks after prot's "return" from K-PAX, Robert Porter was transferred to Ward One.

Epilogue

Robert did fine in One. He got along well with the staff and his fellow patients, expressed normal feelings and desires, was optimistic about his future. In the six weeks he remained there he developed his skills in chess (he even beat Dustin once or twice), studied college catalogs, pursued his interest in biology. His romance with Giselle continued to blossom to the extent that, after three weeks in what he called "Purgatory," I allowed him a weekend furlough in her custody. That worked out quite nicely, and as soon as he was released he moved in with her permanently (along with Oxeye Daisy, their dalmatian).

While Rob was waiting to be discharged, Giselle flew out to Hawaii at her own expense and brought Rob's mother back for a short visit. It was a tearful reunion—his mother hadn't talked with him in more than a decade (she had seen him only in a comatose state). While she was here I spoke with her about Rob's childhood, her husband's fatal accident, etc., as I had five years earlier. Now I learned that Rob's Uncle Dave and Aunt Catherine had died in a fire in 1966, three years after his father's death. Mrs. Porter, of course, had no knowledge of Rob's molestation by them.

She remained in New York only a few days and, buoyed by her happiness at seeing her son nearly ready for discharge, flew back to Honolulu on her own. "It's a shame his father couldn't be here for this," she told me at the airport. "He loved his son very much." I assured her that Robin loved his father, too, though perhaps for more complex reasons than she might have realized.

I think it is safe to say, at last, that all the missing pieces of the puzzle are firmly in place. The root cause of Robert's difficulties lay not, as I had thought, with the terrible tragedy that befell his wife and daughter, but came much earlier, at the hands of a pedophilic uncle. It was this severe trauma that precipitated Rob's abhorrence of sex, and the appearance of an alter (Harry) to help five-year-old Robert deal with the torment.

But why did prot appear on the scene when Robert was six? I believe that Robin felt safe only in the presence of his father, who unwittingly shielded him from the abuse he had experienced at the hands of his Uncle Dave. How devastating it must have been when his "friend and protector" died, leaving him once more at the mercy of that sick creature! Rob called into being a new guardian, one who came from an ideal place where such people as his mother's brother and sister could never exist. Fortunately, Robin wasn't compelled to stay with his aunt and uncle after all, and prot was no longer needed. In fact, it was only after his dog Apple (progenitor of the "aps," the small elephant-like creatures that roam the fields of K-PAX?) was killed that prot made his second appearance on Earth to help Robert, now nine, deal with this new tragedy.

As a result of his traumatic childhood experiences Rob struggled with sex for the rest of his youth and young adulthood, and on into his married life. In sexual matters, prot was virtually useless, and a new identity arose to deal with this problem. Thanks to Paul, Sally was never the wiser, apparently, and they enjoyed a relatively happy life together for several years.

It's not difficult to imagine what Robert must have felt when he came home one fine summer afternoon and found his wife and daughter lying dead on the kitchen floor at the hands of a deranged killer, whose terrible acts brought back his own repressed suffering. Is it any wonder that Harry came to the rescue, that all the pent-up rage he felt for his Uncle Dave exploded like a volcano and he seized the opportunity to prevent this man from performing further atrocities? Or that prot came back to try to help Robert cope with these events, something that perhaps no human being could have done? Indeed, Robert appears to have made an almost miraculous recovery, given the grim circumstances of his tragic background.

Following a trip to Montana (Oxie stayed with us, much to Shasta's delight), Rob enrolled at NYU with a major in field biology. He called me a few weeks later to tell me he was having the time of his life. That's the last I heard of him until the summer of '96, when he and Giselle visited the hospital to renew their acquaintanceship with me and the rest of the staff and patients.

Because so many people had seen prot on television and recognized him wherever Rob went, he had grown a beard. "You'd be surprised," he told me, "how well a beard disguises who you really are." Except for that I found him just as he was when he left, smiling and confident, quite in control. There's a lot of prot in him, I think. But perhaps there's a little of prot in everyone. In any case, he appears to be a fully integrated human being, part of him capable of great things, another part capable of murder.

Giselle's book about prot, *An Alien Among Us?*, came out in December 1996. She reports that it is still selling "spectacularly," and she has been on the talk-show circuit all winter. But the big news, as I write this, is that she is now pregnant, and the baby is due in July. If it is a boy, they tell me they will call him "Gene."

The hospital seems strangely empty without Robert/prot. The patients keep asking when he is coming back, hoping for a ride to the stars. I don't dare tell them that prot gave his life for Robert, and that he is gone for good, because that might make matters worse. And so they wait, and hope, but perhaps this isn't such a bad thing.

Most of our former inmates, however, no longer need prot, and would probably decline a trip to K-PAX even if one was offered. Soon after Bert was discharged he met and married a lovely widow and they legally adopted Jackie, who remained, of course, with us. They visit her regularly, and her new mother is as charming a person as you'd ever want to meet. As a consequence of all this, apparently, Jackie has begun to grow up! It is as if her life was put on hold with the death of her parents, and now that she has a new set, the clock has started ticking again. No one here has ever seen anything quite like it. She even cut off her pigtails!

Lou paid us a visit after her operation. She, too, has found a partner, one who loves her as a woman, and Protista is growing fast. Her first word was (no, not "prot") "cat."

Michael and Manuel and Rudolph are also doing well, all gainfully employed and enjoying their new lives. We hear from them occasionally; they never fail to ask whether prot has returned yet.

Dustin, too, has made spectacular improvement. As a result of my laying down the law to his parents, who now visit him only once a month, he has gradually grown away from coded speeches and game-playing, and has taken an interest in other things. His communications skills have improved accordingly, and I am thinking seriously of moving him to Ward One to see how he gets along there. Incidentally, the purpose of their meeting with me in September was a feeble attempt to learn whether I was on to them, as Will and most of the patients seemed to be.

Others have not done so well. Jerry and his fellow autists remain in their own private worlds, earnestly engineering famous structures and the like. In February, Charlotte, despite being under heavy sedation as an experiment in therapy, nearly castrated and strangled Ron Menninger to death. He is now taking a more cautious approach and there have been no further incidents along that line.

Milton is still trying to cheer us (himself) up with his endless jokes, and Cassandra still sits on the lawn gazing at the stars. She predicted the results of the congressional elections months before voting day, though no one believed her at the time. (I asked her why she hadn't foretold Russell's death and Klaus Villers's suicide. "No one asked me," she replied.) And Frankie, unfortunately, is still Frankie—nasty, foulmouthed, unloved.

The Villerses left their entire estate, valued at several million dollars, to MPI (how they obtained all their wealth remains to be determined). The new wing will be called the Klaus M. and Emma R. Villers Laboratory for Experimental Therapy and Rehabilitation, though the funds won't be released for quite some time, the lawyers tell me. In the meantime, construction costs will be met from other donations and the contributions that came in following prot's television appearance.

Klaus's death left an immense void, of course, which I have tried unsuccessfully to fill. I have had to cut back on the time spent with my patients and take on a lot of onerous duties I could live without. We are currently accepting applications for permanent director, and I, for one, can't wait until the position is filled (Goldfarb and Thorstein are among the candidates).

On a more personal note, my wife will be retiring soon (thanks to the sale of the film rights to *K-PAX*), as will our old friends Bill and Eileen Siegel, who have bought a place in upstate New York and are waiting for Karen and me to join them in an Adirondack retreat of our own. Our son Will graduates from Columbia this spring. He visits the hospital once in a while to keep tabs on the patients and to advise me not to work so hard. I always say, "Tell me that when you're in my shoes!" He is still engaged to Dawn Siegel; they plan to be married "sometime" after they graduate.

Will is as puzzled as I and the rest of the staff by the results of the DNA analyses that came back shortly after Robert was discharged. The laboratory, an extremely reliable one whose clients include some of the country's finest criminologists, reported that Rob's and prot's blood DNA came from two entirely different individuals. Most of us think this must be due to human error, but of course there is no way to prove it.

And then there's the sticky question of how he was able to move, if not at superlight speed, at least fast enough to outrun a TV camera. One physicist estimated that in order to do that he would have to have traveled *at least* twenty-five miles a second, and perhaps much faster.

If that isn't enough, Giselle tells me that prot's trip to the Bronx Zoo provided certain information that no one but zoo officials (and the animals themselves) knew, such things as what their former habitats were like, some foods they missed, and so on. Based on this information, their keepers have tried to replace some of the losses, but I imagine that if prot were still here he would say this misses the point. Happily, the cetologist who visited us has transferred his dolphin, Moby, to a marine biology facility for rehabilitation pending a return to the ocean depths. The young man himself is now selling life insurance.

Regardless of what talents prot may have possessed, however, I still believe that he was nothing more (nor less) than a secondary personality of Robert Porter, and is now an integral part of him. Though many people seem to think he came from K-PAX (including Charlie Flynn, the spider coprophiliac, now mining for gold in the sands of Libya), it seems patently ridiculous to me to imagine that anyone can zip through space on a beam of light without air or heat or protection from various forms of radiation, no matter how fast he travels.

I felt betrayed at first that he "left" us without any warning whatever, especially since he had promised to give me some notice before he departed. But I keep remembering his last words to me in the television studio: "See you later, doc." And that when Robert and Giselle left the hospital to take up their lives elsewhere, Rob gave me a very uncharacteristic wink and Cheshire-cat grin. Moreover, none of the hundred "beings" he planned to take with him has yet disappeared, as far as we know. Is he hiding in Robert's brain somewhere, waiting to come forth again when the time is right?

Or is it possible that he is traveling the Earth at this very moment, searching for unhappy beings to take back to K-PAX with him? For that matter, is there any limit to what is possible? What little we know about life and the universe itself is merely a drop in the ocean of space and time. I still go out at night sometimes and look up at the sky, toward the constellation Lyra. And I still wonder. . . .

ACKNOWLEDGMENTS

I thank my editor, Marc Resnick, for having the good sense to buy this book when others would not.

The Wisdom (or Craziness) of prot

(from his television appearance of Sept. 20, 1995)

Don't blame the politicians for your problems. They are merely a reflection of yourselves.

Many humans feel sorry for the dolphins who are trapped in tuna nets. Who weeps for the tuna?

Your recorded "history" and your "literature" and "art" are merely those of your own species; they ignore all the other beings who share your planet. For a long time we thought that Homo sapiens was the only species living on EARTH.

Religions are difficult for a K-PAXian to understand. Either all of them are right or none of them is.

Human society will always have a drug problem unless life without drugs becomes a more attractive prospect for those concerned.

Hunting is no sport, it is cold-blooded murder. If you can outwrestle a bear or chase down a rabbit, then you can consider yourself a true sportsman.

Killing someone because he killed someone else is an oxymoron.

The root of all evil isn't the lust for money, but money itself. Try to think of a problem that doesn't involve money in some way.

Schools are not for teaching anything. They exist solely to pass on society's beliefs and values to its children.

The purpose of governments is to make your WORLD safe for commerce.

Humans love to fool themselves with euphemisms in order to pretend they aren't eating other animals—"beef" for cow, "pork" for pig, etc. This never fails to elicit gales of laughter from our beings.

All wars are holy wars.

Some humans are concerned with the destruction of their environment and the concomitant extinction of other species. If these well-meaning people were more concerned with the individual beings involved, there would be no need to worry about loss of species.

There will come a time when the human beings of EARTH will be devastated by diseases that will make aids look like a runny nose.

This above all: To thine own WORLD be true.